D0282869

APR 2 3 2019

THE GEMINI MYSTERIES

BOOK ONE
THE NORTH STAR

KAT SHEPHERD

**YELLOW
JACKET**

To Michael, Joanna, Oliver, Leo, and Charlie

The story began with you

—KS

YELLOW JACKET
an imprint of Bonnier Publishing USA

251 Park Avenue South, New York, NY 10010
Text copyright © 2019 by Kat Shepherd
Illustrations copyright © 2019 by Bonnier Publishing USA
All rights reserved, including the right of reproduction in whole or in part in any form.
Yellow Jacket is a trademark of Bonnier Publishing USA, and associated
colophon is a trademark of Bonnier Publishing USA.
Manufactured in the United States
First Edition
1 3 5 7 9 10 8 6 4 2
Library of Congress Cataloging-in-Publication Data is available upon request.
ISBN 978-1-4998-0809-4

yellowjacketreads.com
bonnierpublishingusa.com

CHAPTER
1

Zach Mamuya gripped the steering wheel with both hands and put the pedal to the metal. The shrill whine of the motor cut through the air, and he shot forward, his body slamming against the back of the seat. The yellow go-kart shuddered as he rounded the course's first sharp turn and braced himself, lifting out of the seat and pulling on the wheel hard. He felt the motor rev faster as the ride smoothed out and the kart found its momentum again.

Through his black-and-yellow helmet he heard the buzz of another racer coming up from behind. A neon-green kart was edging forward, its front bumper almost kissing the side of his kart. Number 28. Of course. Zach set his jaw and jerked the wheel to the right, slamming the other racer against the side of the track. He heard the shriek of Number 28's side bumper grinding against the barrier. The friction slowed the other kart down just enough so that Zach could shoot ahead, and he allowed himself a small smile of triumph.

He tore through the track, zipping around a few of the slower racers, until he finally caught up with the royal-blue kart in the lead, Number 17. Zach's grin widened. He had raced against 17 before. Piece of cake. The blue kart was playing it safe, filling out the middle of the track to hedge against anyone passing him on either side. Zach tested the other driver, edging up on his left side. The blue racer responded by pulling to the left and blocking him, as Zach expected he would. Zach stayed right behind him, easing up on the accelerator, and waited for his chance. Just ahead he knew the track began a long, smooth curve to the right. His timing would have to be perfect.

Right before the curve, Zach darted to the left and tapped Number 17's left bumper. The driver responded just as he had before, by pulling left to block the pass.

Zach laughed and hit the accelerator hard, pulling his steering wheel to the right. By goading the other driver into blocking the outside of the track's turn, Zach had just claimed the inside of the curve, which would shave precious milliseconds off his lap time. He pulled the wheel to the right, preparing to speed forward and dominate the track.

A blur of neon green filled the right side of his vision. Number 28. The green kart's left bumper grazed his and pushed him into the blue kart, tangling them together as Number 28 shot forward. The green racer hugged the inside of the curve like a pro, streaking through the turn. Zach pulled to the right and followed, taking the inside of the turn and edging past 17, but the victory felt hollow. There's no way he'd be able to beat 28's time on that lap.

Zach shook his head as he passed the finish line and pulled into the bay. He unbuckled his harness belt and stepped out of the go-kart. He joined the other racers as they headed over to the board to check their official times. Just as he'd suspected: second place.

Zach pulled off his helmet and mask, and walked

over to 28. "Nice move," he said, holding out his fist for a bump.

His twin sister, Evie, slipped off her gear, revealing shoulder-length braids and light-brown skin dusted with freckles. "I know," she said, bumping him back and exploding her fist out.

"Where'd you pick up that little trick anyway?" he asked. "YouTube?"

Evie laughed. "Dream on, bro! I don't cop anyone's style!"

The blue kart racer took off his helmet, and a grinning Vishal Desai punched Evie lightly on the arm. "I see Evie's as humble as always."

Evie brushed imaginary lint off of her shoulder. "I can't help it if you two can't keep up!"

Zach's eyes widened in disbelief. "As if! I left you in the dust back there, remember? I still don't know how you caught up with me."

"How I *won*, you mean? Maybe if you hadn't counted me out so fast, you would have remembered to watch your back. Vishal's not the only one to beat around here."

Zach held up his helmet. "Care for another round? We'll see who's still talking trash after that."

Evie looked at her watch. "Mom said we have to meet her outside by 7:30, so you'll just have to wait 'til next time to lose to me again."

Vishal glanced between the two siblings. "Seriously. Do you two ever stop competing with each other?"

Zach and Evie looked at each other. "No," they said at the same time. The twins high-fived and headed to the counter to return their helmets.

"I'm so glad I'm an only child," Vishal muttered, following behind them.

***

Sophia Boyd couldn't understand how a perfect evening could go so wrong. She watched her mother fumble to put an earring in her left ear while cradling a cell phone against her right.

Mareva's voice betrayed a hint of rising panic as she spoke to the other person on the line. "What do you mean, stuck in traffic? This is Minneapolis, not New York; we don't have traffic! The party starts in twenty minutes!"

Dashiell Boyd paced the floor of their bedroom. "You've got to be kidding me. We hired this event planner months ago to make sure that everything went smoothly tonight. And now she might not even make the party?" He ran his hand through his graying hair.

Mareva balanced against the wall and stepped into a pair of sky-high heels. "A flash mob? I don't even know what that is," she said into the phone. The Boyds walked through the hallway and down the grand staircase to a massive living room that opened onto a sweeping stone patio. The furniture had been removed, and the room converted into a ballroom for the evening, with a bar in the corner and a small stage set up at one end of the room.

Sophia bent over the box of floral centerpieces and grabbed an armful to place on the tall, narrow cocktail tables scattered throughout the room.

"That's the spirit, Soph," her dad said approvingly. "It may not exactly be the night you dreamed of, but if we all pitch in, I bet everything will go just fine."

"I hope so," Sophia said nervously. "All the guests

did RSVP, right?" Sophia didn't even know why she was asking; she had checked the guest list dozens of times. She could practically recite every name in her sleep.

"Well, there is one small change," Dashiell said. "Your mom's aunt Marguerite called earlier today and said she's not feeling well, so she can't make it."

"But she was so looking forward to tonight!" Sophia cried.

"I know, sweetie. She was really disappointed."

"Well, I guess at least it means that leech Evan Masterson won't be here, either, then," Sophia said.

Dashiell tried to look stern. "Now, come on, Soph, I know you don't like the guy, but calling him a leech may be going a little too far."

"Yeah, right, Dad. I've heard you and Mom talk about him. You know he's only after Aunt Marguerite for her money; the guy's at least thirty years younger than she is! Every time he comes over he looks like he's casing the place. He gives me the creeps."

"Well, whatever we think of him, he's still Marguerite's friend, so we have to be polite."

Dashiell saw Sophia's sullen expression and lowered his voice. "But between you and me, kid, I wouldn't worry too much. Your mom had a quiet word with her aunt about Evan a few weeks ago. Let's just say I don't think Marguerite will be putting him into her will anytime soon."

"Thanks, Dad." Sophia rested her head on her dad's shoulder for a moment before pulling out her phone and checking the evening's to-do list. "Okay, so the centerpieces are ready, and the string quartet will be set up here once they finish tuning up." She pointed to a small cluster of chairs and music stands on the stage. "What about the food and drinks?"

"Tell you what, I'll go make sure the bartender remembers to bring up an extra case of champagne, and then we'll tackle the kitchen." Dashiell straightened his cuff links and disappeared through the door to the dining room.

Mareva let out a loud sigh into the phone. "Yes, of course we have the schedule you made for tonight. I'll have Sophia print it out and make sure every staff member has a copy. You're sure everyone knows what to do?" Mareva looked around the ballroom wearily. "Okay, well, we'll do our best."

Sophia could hear the event planner's muffled voice through the phone. The tone was calm and reassuring, and Sophia rolled her eyes. As if. Like anyone was going to feel calm when their event planner canceled less than an hour before what was supposed to be one of the most important parties of the year.

Sophia's parents were well-known philanthropists, and she had been dragged along to charity fund-raisers for as long as she could remember. But tonight was supposed to be different. Sophia wasn't being dragged to this one; she was the one who convinced her parents to throw the event in the first place.

In sixth grade last year, Sophia had been assigned a report on gibbons. She hadn't even known what a gibbon was when she started, but she quickly fell in love with the adorable primates and was horrified to discover that they were some of the most endangered animals on the planet. When she learned that the Minneapolis Zoo was hoping to build an education center and exhibit to house a pair of critically endangered gibbons, she begged her parents to lead the fund-raising efforts. Tonight was supposed to be the kickoff.

Mareva hung up the phone and turned to her daughter. "Sophia, can you—"

Sophia held up a manila folder filled with copies of the evening's schedule. "Already on it, Mom."

"You're a dream." Mareva straightened the top of her strapless black gown. Her neckline was bare, her hair pulled back into an elegant chignon at the back of her head. "Do I look too plain? I don't want anything to take away from the North Star once I put it on. It is, after all, the guest of honor."

CHAPTER
2

Sophia smiled at her mother. "Mom, every person at the party is going to want to bid on that necklace once they see you wearing it. It'll be perfect." Sophia hugged her mom and looked up at her anxiously. "Are you sure you're okay with this? I know it's been in your family for generations."

Mareva stroked her daughter's hair. "Honey, we've always told you that the North Star would be yours someday. I couldn't be prouder to know that you're willing to give it up for something you care about. That family legacy means much more to me than diamonds." She picked up a centerpiece and shooed her daughter toward the kitchen. "Now, let's go make sure this party doesn't fall apart before it even starts!"

Sophia hurried off to the kitchen to pass schedules out to the staff. The caterers hired for the evening bustled around her, piling silver trays high with delectable treats. In the corner of the kitchen, the bartender and chef were arguing about wine pairings.

Sophia heard the doorbell ring and glanced at the clock. The first guests were already arriving! She rushed to answer the front door, but her mother was already there, greeting an older woman in a long, burgundy velvet dress and elbow-length gloves that highlighted her mahogany skin. The woman's ears and throat were dripping with jewels. Mareva saw Sophia and beckoned her over. "Darling, come and meet Gwendolyn Fairbanks! Your father and I saw her sing *Aida* at the Minnesota Opera just before you were born!"

Sophia reached to shake Gwendolyn's hand, and the opera singer presented hers palm down, almost like she expected Sophia to kiss it. Sophia glanced quickly at Mareva, but saw no guidance in her mother's frozen smile. There seemed to be a small undercurrent of tension between the two women that Sophia couldn't quite read. Sophia squeezed the opera singer's hand between both of hers. "How lovely to meet you! Thank you for coming."

Gwendolyn stepped inside and looked imperiously around the foyer. "I thought tonight's soiree was to be a preview for those who wish to bid on the North Star, but I don't see it anywhere. How are potential buyers supposed to know what they're bidding on if you're keeping it locked away somewhere?"

Mareva's hand flew to her throat. "Oh, goodness! Things were so busy I forgot to put it on!" She turned toward the staircase, but just at that moment, a crash came from the hallway. "Oh, what now?" Mareva mumbled, and rushed off to investigate.

Sophia gave Gwendolyn her most dazzling smile and took her elbow, leading her to a table laden with cheese and fruit. "Thank you again for coming. Would you like some champagne?" Gwendolyn nodded stiffly, and Sophia turned to the kitchen, nearly colliding with her mother, who was rushing to answer the doorbell again.

"One of the waitstaff fell and twisted her ankle, so now we're one down. Luckily she'll be all right, but I've got her set up in the pantry with some frozen peas on her ankle. Could you pass a tray for a few minutes while I get the door?" Without waiting for an answer, Mareva made a beeline for the foyer to greet the small handful of new guests that were streaming through the doorway.

Sophia waved to her father, who was standing behind the bar serving a cocktail to a sallow, dour-looking man in a brown suit. "I would have thought that you would have a *professional* bartender," the man said peevishly.

Sophia's father forced a smile. "He'll be along in a sec." He turned to his daughter. "Sophia, can you check with the bartender while you're back there?"

"I'm on it!" she called back. On her way to the kitchen, she recognized a young couple talking with Gwendolyn Fairbanks: Gideon Doheny and his fiancée, Abigail Morris. Gideon had a perfect tan and dazzlingly white teeth. He sported a pink shirt under his suit jacket, and Abigail wore a nervous smile and a huge diamond on her left hand. Just then, Gideon's cell phone rang, and he held up one finger. "I'm sorry; I have to take this." He excused himself and walked away from the group, leaving the two women in uncomfortable silence.

From across the room Sophia heard a loud whooping. Social media celebrity Jasmine Jetani was holding up a glass of champagne and Snapchatting against a backdrop of stuffy old people with disapproving looks on their faces. Her fake eyelashes fluttered, and her glossy pink lips pouted into the camera. "Woo-hoo! Better get ready, peeps, because in a few days this famous neck is going to be draped in the most legendary diamonds in Minneapolis! It's gonna be epic!"

Jasmine threw her arm up in the air, spilling champagne all over her pink sequined minidress and splashing her marabou-trimmed heels. She shrieked and switched off the phone's camera. "These shoes are one of a kind!" She looked around, and her eyes fell on Sophia. Jasmine hurried over and grabbed her arm. "Where's your bathroom?"

Sophia wordlessly pointed down the back hall.

Returning to the kitchen, Sophia steeled herself, trying to channel her inner Mareva. Sophia's mother was an attorney who had taken on a lot of highly contentious court cases. Surely Sophia could find a way to keep the bartender and chef from killing one another, assuming she could get them to listen to a thirteen-year-old.

After a few minutes of flattery combined with her biggest puppy-dog brown eyes, Sophia managed to get the bartender back to his post and the chef focused on the next round of hors d'oeuvres.

A caterer came back to the kitchen with an empty tray. "We're in the weeds out there," she said breathlessly. "It's like these folks have never eaten before! I can't keep up!"

Sophia held out her arms. "I'll take a tray." The caterer looked at the chef, who nodded, and handed Sophia a silver tray of toast points and caviar.

Sophia brought the tray to a group of white-haired old ladies. "Oh, how sweet," one lady said. "Isn't it lovely how you're helping out Mommy and Daddy tonight when I'm sure you'd rather be watching video games like all the other children?"

Sophia forced a smile and passed around the tray of caviar. "Well, actually, this gibbon fund-raiser was my idea. See, there's this stuff called palm oil. It's in everything from lotion to peanut butter, and because of it, gibbons are losing their habitat."

She looked earnestly at the group, who was munching their toast, crumbs drifting down their chins, but the women's attention had already wandered. One of them pointed across the room. "Oh, look! Isn't that Gladys Ganje? Why, I think she's had a face-lift!"

Sophia took a deep breath and looked around the room. She saw her mother heading up the grand staircase, and the two shared a smile before Mareva disappeared down the hallway. Sophia moved to a group of silver-haired men. She offered the tray.

"Why, look at you!" one of the men said. "Aren't your parents lucky to have such a pretty little helper? I bet you wish you were out on a date instead of at this boring old party. Your father must already be chasing the boys away!"

Sophia gritted her teeth and tried to ignore her rising frustration. "Thank you for coming tonight. The gibbons really need your help. Did you know that over three hundred football fields of rain forest are destroyed *every hour* to make palm oil plantations? If we don't do something, gibbons could become extinct, along with a lot of other animals."

One of the men turned to the others. "Speaking of football, did you all catch the Vikings game last Sunday? What a nail-biter!"

Sophia started back toward the kitchen and was pounced upon by Gwendolyn. "Not so fast," the opera singer said. "I haven't had any yet!" Gwendolyn reached for a corner of toast and spread it liberally with caviar. The tray was heavy; Sophia's arms were beginning to ache. Gwendolyn reached for a second triangle of toast and dug the spoon even deeper into the pot of caviar. Sophia's patient smile felt frozen on her face. She shifted her weight from one foot to the other and looked at the clock on the wall.

That's when she heard her mother scream.

***

Sophia dropped the tray, and caviar and toast went flying. Gwendolyn recoiled, but it was too late. "My gown!" Caviar clung to her velvet dress.

"I'm sorry!" Sophia called over her shoulder, already

running toward the stairs. The party guests murmured to one another, their eyebrows raised in consternation. A few of the white-haired old ladies hovered around Gwendolyn, clucking like a group of hens and dabbing at her with the lace hankies they kept in their sleeves.

When Sophia reached the top of the staircase, she raced down the hall to her parents' room. Their house manager, Maurice, was standing in the doorway. "Maurice!" Sophia cried. "What's going on? Is my mom okay?"

She tried to enter the room, but Maurice blocked the door. "Your mom's fine, Soph. Don't worry."

"Yeah, but what happened? Why did she scream?" Sophia pushed forward, but Maurice wouldn't let her through. "Maurice, you're blocking the door. Why can't I go in?" She craned to see around Maurice's brawny shoulder and saw her mom kneeling on the floor of the closet, barefoot. Her perfect chignon was disheveled, and her eye makeup was smudged. Sophia's father had his arm around her and held his cell phone to his ear.

"Sorry, Soph, but nobody can go in here right now.

Your parents will be down in a few minutes, and they'll explain everything. For now, the best thing you can do is go back downstairs and focus on making sure that everyone at the party has a good time. Tell the catering staff to send out some extra rounds of champagne or something, okay?" He gave her an encouraging smile. "After all, I know this is a big night for you. We don't want anyone leaving too soon!"

Sophia searched his face. "No, I guess not," she said finally. "You promise they're okay? And they'll be down in a few minutes?"

Maurice's face was a careful mask. "I promise you that neither of your parents is injured in any way. They'll join you just as soon as they can."

Sophia narrowed her eyes. "That was kind of a weird answer, Maurice."

He shrugged noncommittally.

"I wish you'd just tell me what's going on."

Maurice shrugged again. "Sorry, Soph, I can't right now." But it didn't matter if he told her what happened or not.

She already knew.

***

Evie Mamuya sat in the front seat of her mom's gray Prius, still glowing from her racing victory. Behind her, Zach and Vishal debated the relative merits of pizza versus burgers for dinner.

"I am so down for a Juicy Lucy right now. The cheese is *inside the burger*. It's off the hook!"

"Dude, pizza all the way! You know I don't eat beef," Vishal said.

"Maybe the winner should get to decide where we eat dinner," Evie said over her shoulder. "Just sayin'."

Mrs. Mamuya laughed. "You're really going to milk this thing, aren't you?"

Evie grinned. "You know it, Mom!"

Zach leaned forward between the two seats. "Don't get too comfortable in the winner's seat. Remember, there's still mini golf."

Evie cracked her knuckles. "I'm not worried."

"Yeah, well, maybe you should be. Remember, I am the undefeated mini-golf champ in the state of Massachusetts!" Vishal folded his arms and smirked.

Zach gave him a playful shove. "Get over yourself!

The only people you've played against in Massachusetts are your grandparents!"

"Every time we visit my grandparents, we play mini golf, and every time, I win. Which means that I have never been defeated in the state of Massachusetts." Vishal raised both arms in triumph. "*Boom!* Undefeated."

Suddenly, Mrs. Mamuya's phone crackled to life. "Hang on a sec, guys. It's the scanner app."

The kids quieted down. Mrs. Mamuya was a crime reporter for the *Minneapolis Telegraph*. The scanner app on her phone allowed her to hear real-time police radio calls so she wouldn't miss any potential big stories. *"Squad 520, please respond to 1621 West Upton Place. Report of possible 10-82, with a potential 10-77 still in the area. Please 10-25 Dashiell Boyd at location."*

Mrs. Mamuya flipped on her turn signal and headed toward Kenwood. "Sorry, everybody. Mini golf is going to have to wait."

MINNESOTA POLICE CODES

10-5 Relay
10-6 Busy, Will Call
10-7 Out Of Service
10-8 In Service
10-9 Repeat Message
10-14 Convoy Or Escort
10-15 Prisoner In Custody
10-16 Daily Reports
10-19 Return To Station
10-20 Location
10-25 Have Contact With
10-26 Call Office
10-29 Check For Stolen/Wanted
10-32 Breathalyzer Available
10-33 Emergency Traffic
10-34 Trouble At Station
10-35 Confidential Information
10-36 Correct Time
10-38 Investigating
10-39 Assist Officer At
10-40 Do Not Divulge Loc.
10-41 Switch To Channel #
10-42 Call Home
10-47 Urinalysis Report
10-48 Blood Alcohol Report

10-52 Personal Injury Accident
10-53 10-52 & EMS Enroute
10-54 Fatality Accident
10-55 Funeral
10-57 Intoxicated/Inebriated
10-72 Dead Person (DOA)
10-73 Abandoned Vehicle
10-74 Theft
10-75 Juvenile Trouble
10-77 Prowler
10-TS Ambulance/EMS Call
10-79 Domestic Disturbance
10-80 Sex Crime
10-81 ADT Or Bank
10-82 Burglary
10-83 Disturbance
10-84 Fight
10-85 Knifing/Stabbing
10-86 Armed Robbery (Holdup)
10-87 Shooting
10-88 Officer Needs Help
10-89 Homicide
10-95 Radio Check
10-96 Civil Defense "Alert"
10-97 Civil Defense "Evacuate"

CHAPTER
3

Evie turned around in her seat and waggled her eyebrows at the two boys. "What do you think happened? Maybe we'll get to help catch the perp!"

Mrs. Mamuya laughed. "Relax, Evie. It's just a burglary; they think a prowler could still be in the area, but I'm sure the thief is probably long gone by now. The big story isn't the burglary; it's what they stole. I have a hunch it's the North Star necklace."

"Weren't they going to auction that off at the Gibbon Gala next week?" Evie asked.

"Exactly," her mother answered. "They were hosting a party tonight for bidders to preview the diamonds. Without the North Star, the zoo is going to have a hard time raising the funds they need. This is a story that could impact the whole city."

Mrs. Mamuya parked the car on a side street and grabbed her work bag. She paused to slip on a dark gray blazer she kept in her trunk and smooth her short ash-blond hair. The kids followed her past a neatly parked line of luxury cars and down a long, gated driveway. The gate was open, and there was a squad car parked next to the temporary valet stand that was set up near the front entrance.

Evie paused in the driveway, taking in the sprawling stone mansion and its ivy-covered walls. The house and immaculate grounds were lit with strategically placed spotlights that bathed the walled estate in a saffron glow. Several shallow steps led up to a wide stone patio bordered by a low wall, where a police officer was attempting to corral a group of querulous guests back into the house.

Mrs. Mamuya turned to the kids. "Wait outside, okay? The house could still be a crime scene, and the police won't want a bunch of new people coming in and touching everything. I have my cell, so call if you need something or want me to get you a car service. It could be a long night." Mrs. Mamuya waved and reached into the blazer pocket where she kept her press credentials, walking confidently toward the officer in charge.

Zach pulled his phone out of his pocket. "So, what are we supposed to do while we wait?" He flicked idly through his game apps.

Evie scanned the sweeping front yard. The expanse of grass between the crescent-shaped driveway and the street was dotted with a few tall trees, but there were few shadows or interesting spots to explore. She noticed some hedges near the side of the house that led to the back. "Let's go check out the backyard," she suggested.

"Good idea," Vishal said. "It's gotta be sweet back there. I wonder if they have a tennis court." He hopped over the patio wall and slipped through the bushes. "Come on!" Evie jumped down after him.

Zach hung back. "What if the thief is hiding back there?"

Vishal gestured dismissively. "Nobody's going to steal a diamond necklace and then hang around waiting to get caught. There's like a million people here!"

Zach cast a nervous glance behind him and joined the others. The three kept close to the side of the house, avoiding the open windows where they could see guests peering out into the shadowy gardens. A man in a sharp suit and a pink shirt leaned casually against the windowsill, holding a cocktail in his hand. He turned to his companions, his brash voice cutting the air. "The police can't possibly suspect any of the guests! Why would any of *us* steal the North Star? I could buy a hundred of them without even breaking a sweat!" He guffawed loudly at his own witticism. Zach rolled his eyes. Who was this guy kidding? That laugh sounded fake even to him.

The kids reached the back of the house, where a broad flagstone patio overlooked a sparkling swimming pool flanked by formal gardens on either side. Beyond was an expansive stretch of grassy lawn and a tennis court. "I knew it!" Vishal said. He pulled a tennis ball out of his pocket. "Do you want to play?"

"How?" Evie asked. "We don't have any rackets."

Vishal tossed the ball in the air. "We could figure something out."

Zach grinned. "Another of your famous Desai Games?" He held out his hands for a catch.

Vishal threw him the ball. "I've got some ideas." Never one to sit around bored, Vishal could turn anything into a game. His closet was crammed with homemade board games and a variety of balls and equipment for various new "sports" he had invented.

Zach threw the ball back, but the pitch went wild, sailing over Vishal's head and into the formal gardens. "Sorry," Zach called.

"I'll get it," Vishal said. He vaulted over a carved stone bench, barely avoiding a pedestal that held a bonsai tree in an ornamental pot. "This would make a great obstacle course!" He squeezed between two rosebushes and knelt to retrieve the ball, then shimmied back between the rosebushes and carefully edged around the bonsai. He was just preparing to hop back over the bench, when something shiny caught his eye. "What's this doing here?"

CHAPTER
4

"What's a hockey puck doing in the middle of a garden?" Vishal asked.

Zach shrugged. "Maybe they have a hockey rink."

Vishal looked around. "Where?"

"Our cousins in Milwaukee have a basketball court that they turn into a hockey rink in the winter. Maybe they do that with the tennis court," Evie suggested.

"Maybe." Vishal picked up the puck and turned it over in his hands. "It's heavy, though. And why is it silver?"

Zach's face brightened. "Maybe it's some kind of electronic hockey. Dude, that would be so awesome!"

Vishal slipped the puck into his pocket. "Oh, man. Just imagine what the sticks would be like!"

"Hey!" The kids looked up to see a girl their age

glowering down on them from the patio railing. She had light-olive skin and wore a simple, above-the-knee dress with spaghetti straps, and her dark bobbed hair swung forward, obscuring her face. She paused to tuck her hair behind her ear, her dark eyes narrowing under her blunt-cut bangs. "What are you doing in my yard? *You* weren't invited!"

Evie's heart sank. Sophia Boyd. Evie didn't really know her, but she recognized her from school. Sophia had transferred in from some private school last year and had made a huge deal about her parents sending her to public school to have a more "enrichingly authentic educational experience," or something like that. Evie was a friendly girl, but even friendliness had its limits.

Flustered at being caught out, Evie decided to bluff. She stood up straighter. "How do you know we weren't invited? It's your parents' party, not yours!"

Sophia sighed in exasperation. "Why does everyone keep saying that?" She marched down the patio steps, her kitten heels echoing on the stone. "Look, this party was *my idea*! I know every name on that guest list, and believe me, yours wasn't on it, and neither were your parents'. Besides, even if I hadn't planned this party, I'm not an idiot." Her eyes raked across the three kids, taking in their jeans and T-shirts. "You wouldn't have made it through the front door dressed like that."

Evie felt her cheeks growing warm. She struggled to find something to say, but it was Zach's voice, not hers, that cut the awkward silence.

"Sorry. Our bad." Zach flashed a sheepish, easygoing smile, and Evie saw Sophia's expression soften. Not much, but a little. "I'm Zach, and this is my twin sister, Evie, and our friend Vishal. Our mom writes for the *Telegraph*, and she got the call to cover a story, so we kind of got dragged along. We were just going to hang out in the yard to keep out of the way." He rubbed the back of his neck. "I hope we didn't scare you or anything."

"I wasn't scared," Sophia said stiffly. "I just came outside to get some air and I saw you down here." She looked down at her feet. "I was hoping you might have been the thieves, and then maybe this whole nightmare could be over."

"So then the North Star really was taken?" Evie asked softly.

Sophia nodded miserably, her eyes filling with tears.

"I'm sorry," Evie said. "I know the necklace has been in your family a long time."

Sophia wiped her tears away angrily. "I don't care at all about that. It's just a stupid necklace! I'm worried about the gibbons! What's going to happen to them now?" She pulled a crumpled tissue out of her pocket and blew her nose. "I mean, what kind of jerk person would steal something from a *charity* event?"

"What happened, exactly?" Vishal asked. "How did it get stolen?"

Sophia took a deep breath. "Nobody knows yet." She led the others up the steps to the patio. "My mom had it on earlier today when she was choosing her gown, but she put it back in the safe shortly before the party started. Our event planner didn't show up, so things were running behind, and she forgot to put it back on. About an hour into the party, she went upstairs to get the North Star, but when she opened the safe, it was gone."

Vishal bounced his tennis ball on the patio, thinking. "So the safe wasn't broken into?"

Sophia shook her head. "My mom unlocked it herself, just like always."

Zach held out his hands and Vishal bounced him the ball. He caught it easily and threw it back to Vishal. "So whoever stole the North Star knows the combination to your safe."

Sophia nodded. "But that's the weird part. Only three people know the combination to the safe: my dad, my mom, and Maurice." She pointed to herself. "Even *I* don't know it!"

Evie held out her hand, and Vishal tossed the ball to her. "Hold up, who's Maurice?"

She bounced the ball to Sophia, who missed it. It rolled under a wrought-iron table, and Sophia crouched down and reached under the table. "He's our house manager." The other kids looked blankly at her. "A big house like this needs constant attention and takes, like, a staff of people to keep it running," she explained. "Maurice makes it all work." She bounced the ball and caught it.

Zach looked at the others before he spoke, his voice cautious. "I mean, is there any chance that Maurice—?"

"No!" Sophia cut him off sharply. "I've known Maurice since I was *born*. He's like family. He taught me how to ride a bike, okay? There is no way he would do this."

"Sorry," Zach said, "but I had to ask."

"Yeah, well, so did the police," Sophia answered bitterly. "They asked, and asked, and *asked*. They're convinced Maurice must have done it, or that he slipped and told some other staff member the combination. Like he would ever do that!" She threw the ball hard against the ground, and it bounced high in the air. She caught it on its way back down. "The cops aren't even *looking* at any of the guests!" Sophia tossed the ball to Vishal and sat down on one of the patio chairs. "They asked to search one woman's bag, and she made such a stink about it that they totally backed down."

Evie sat in the chair next to Sophia's. "But how would someone be able to open the safe if they didn't know the combination?"

Sophia shrugged. "I don't know, but there has to be a way."

Vishal slouched into a lounge chair. "So if there *were* some way that someone else got the combination to the safe, then it could be anyone, right? What makes you think it was a guest?"

Sophia leaned forward, her dark eyes intent. "Look, the only time my parents' room was left empty was between seven and eight. I was in charge of passing out the party planner's schedule, and I know for a fact that every single staff member had a job and place to be in that first hour. If they hadn't been in their position, somebody would have *noticed*."

"But why would a *guest* steal the necklace?" Zach asked. "Everybody here is rich. They could just buy it."

"That's exactly what the cops said!" Sophia threw herself back in her chair. "Seriously, doesn't anyone around here have any imagination?" She folded her arms. "Look, one of the main reasons I transferred to public school was because my parents were worried about 'bad influences.' Half the girls at my old school had been arrested for shoplifting before they even got to high school. These were kids who could literally buy anything they wanted already."

Evie bit her lip. "Yeah, but there's always stuff your parents won't let you get."

Sophia gave a wry smile and shook her head. "This one girl, Sadie . . . for her birthday weekend, her parents took her and her friends on a shopping trip. *In Dubai.* Two weeks later, I see her at Bloomingdale's getting busted for stealing a bottle of perfume."

Zach leaned his elbows on the patio railing and rested his head in his hands. "Rich people are weird." He looked back at Sophia. "Oh. Sorry. I didn't mean you or anything."

Sophia shrugged. "Don't worry about it."

Suddenly, Zach leaned forward and peered into the darkness beyond the patio. He beckoned silently with his arm, and the others joined him. He pointed down to the garden and dropped his voice to a whisper. "Don't look now, but I think someone's spying on us."

CHAPTER
5

"I bet it's the thief!" Vishal said softly. "Maybe we can surprise him. Come on!"

"Hold up a sec," Zach whispered. "We need a plan."

"No time for that!" Vishal threw his leg over the railing and dropped softly as a cat onto the lawn below. Evie followed.

Sophia kicked off her heels and ran barefoot down the steps. Zach hesitated for a moment before hurrying down the steps after Sophia. "This is a very bad idea," he mumbled to himself.

The four met up under a tree near where the spy was hiding. "Okay, so what do we do now?" Zach asked.

"I say we rush the hedge and grab him!" Evie said.

"No way," Zach argued. "He could be armed. One

of us should go and get the cops while the others keep an eye on him."

"Oh, sure. Because if there's one thing cops always do, it's listen to brown kids like us," Vishal said sarcastically.

"What do you think, Sophia?" Zach turned to look for her, but she was gone. "Oh no!" He grabbed Vishal's wrist and pointed. Sophia had her back against the hedge and was creeping sideways toward the spy's hiding spot.

"Fan out," Evie whispered. "Let's try to surround him." She dropped to her hands and knees and slithered under the hedge to the other side.

Zach threw up his hands in frustration. "Seriously, Vish. Are we the only ones around here with any sense of self-preservation whatsoever?!" Vishal was gone, too. Zach looked back at the house. Should he go get someone?

Just then, there was a rustling in the hedge and a loud crash of branches. Sophia screamed and jumped back as someone exploded out of the hedge. A shadowy figure knocked Zach to the ground.

Zach grabbed the intruder's ankle, tripping him. The intruder stumbled and fell onto one knee, but before Zach could get up the man recovered and broke into a lurching run. Zach heard shouts and more crashing as Evie and Vishal searched for a way through the hedge.

Sophia took off after the intruder. Zach struggled to his feet and followed, but by the time he caught up, Sophia stood alone in the clearing. The intruder had disappeared.

Still panting, Zach bent at the waist and checked himself for injury. No tears in his pants, and no blood. Good. He brushed a few leaves off of the sleeve of his navy-blue fleece.

Sophia paced the clearing, her bare feet streaked with mud and wet grass. "I can't believe he got away. Did you get a good look at him?"

Zach shook his head. "He had on a hooded jacket, so I only caught a glimpse of his face."

"What did he look like?" Sophia asked.

"White guy. Light eyes. That's about all I could see."

Sophia nodded. "Sounds about right."

Zach's eyes widened. "Do you know who it is?"

Sophia shrugged uncertainly. "I didn't get a good view, either, but it kind of looked like my great-aunt's 'friend,' Evan Masterson." She put air quotes around *friend*, her voice dripping with sarcasm at the word. "He's, like, thirty years younger than she is. He's a tennis instructor at the country club." She rolled her eyes. "So predictable. You know how the rest goes."

Zach most emphatically did not know, but he nodded politely and tried to look worldly and wise. "Yeah, sure. Of course." He made a mental note to ask Evie about it later.

Evie and Vishal jogged up. "Sorry," Evie said. "It took us a few minutes to get through the hedge." She picked at the twigs stuck in her braids and grimaced. "My girl at the salon is going to kill me." She peered into the shadows of the side yard. "You lost him?"

Zach nodded. "But Sophia thinks she might know who it was."

Sophia filled Vishal and Evie in on her suspicions.

"But why would this Evan Masterson guy be hiding out here? Wasn't he invited to the party anyway?" Evie asked.

"Exactly," Sophia said triumphantly. "I bet you anything he stole the North Star. Why else would he be out here lurking around like some creepy . . . lurker?"

A smile played at the corner of Vishal's mouth. "Yeah, the whole lurking thing is def suspicious. Except that, you know, you also caught *us* in your garden."

"Yeah, well, you weren't *lurking*," Sophia said huffily. "Come on." She scanned the ground. "We have to find some clue that will prove what Evan was up to."

The group searched for clues. They rounded a corner, and Sophia pointed at something near the house. "I knew it!" She hopped gingerly across the gravel path, yelping as the hard stones dug into the soles of her bare feet. She crouched down next to a broken ornamental pot and looked up at the others, her eyes shining. "See? This isn't supposed to be here. Look at the drag marks." The heavy pot had left a trail of matted, scuffed grass in its wake where it had been dragged from the patio nearby.

The others bent down and took a closer look. The blue-and-white pot was enormous, at least four feet tall; it lay on its side in two jagged pieces. Sophia pointed up to the open second-floor window directly above. "That's my mother's dressing room. Evan must have dragged the pot under here and used it to get through the window. That's why he was hanging around in the yard. I bet he was planning to put the pot back to cover his tracks."

"Maybe," Zach said, looking at the window high above. "But that's a really long drop. Even with the pot's help he'd have to be, like, a ninja to get up there."

Evie pointed at a nearby patch of soft mud. Footsteps led away from the pot and back to the party. "Somebody was here all right, but it wasn't the person hiding in the hedge."

CHAPTER
6

"Unless the intruder changed his shoes before hiding in the hedges, then these footprints don't belong to the person we chased through the garden," Evie continued. "The shape of the shoe print is totally different."

Sophia sighed in frustration. "I need to get back to the party." She looked down at her dirty feet, her shoulders hunched in failure. "Not that there's any point to it now. With the North Star gone, there won't be anything to bid on at the auction next Saturday." She trudged back toward the house, the others in tow.

Zach exchanged glances with Evie and Vishal, and when he spoke, his voice was filled with bravado. "Don't give up so soon. We're gonna get that necklace back for you." He nudged the other two. "Right?"

Evie looked startled, but she flashed a confident smile. "Oh, yeah. Totally!"

Vishal caught the mood. "No doubt!" He jumped up to touch a tree branch as they passed under it, and when he landed, he put some extra swagger in his step.

When the group returned to the patio, Sophia hosed off her dirty feet and dried them on a fluffy beach towel from a bin near the pool. She stepped back into her shoes and led the others inside to the drawing room, where the party guests sat wearily, waiting to have their individual names and statements taken down by the uniformed officer seated at a table in the corner.

Sophia tapped the officer's shoulder. "Excuse me." The officer ignored her and continued writing down answers in his slow block print. Sophia tapped again. "Excuse me!"

The officer sighed and looked up. "Now you've gone and made me lose my place. What can I do for you, little girl?"

Sophia leaned forward and dropped her voice. "These kids and I were just outside and we saw an intruder, and I'm fairly certain it's the perpetrator. I suggest you and your fellow officers go check it out."

The officer rolled his eyes. "Very funny. Now if you don't mind, I have *real* work to do."

Sophia's face was tense, and her voice rose. "I assure you, officer, this is no joke. Please hurry! He's probably getting away as we speak!" She pointed to the French doors that led outside.

The officer stood up, and a look of relief passed over Sophia's face. But instead of taking action, he folded his arms and glowered. "Now, listen, kid, I've tried to be nice. I don't know who you think you are, but a very serious crime has been committed. So go find your mommy and daddy and don't bother me again."

Sophia drew herself up to her full height. "Do you have any idea who I am? I'm Sophia Boyd, and this is my house! Perhaps you'd feel more comfortable speaking with my *father*, Dashiell Boyd?"

The officer blanched. "I'm sorry, Miss Boyd, we'll check it out right away." He fumbled for his radio and mumbled into it. He turned back to Sophia. "We sent some officers to take a look. Is there anything else?"

Sophia declined and turned away, her hair whipping

around her face. The other kids gaped at her. "Wow," Vishal said. "If I said that to a cop, I'm pretty sure he wouldn't have acted like that."

Sophia shrugged. "The police are here to protect and serve, aren't they?" Vishal and the twins just looked at each other.

Zach tapped Sophia's elbow. "In the meantime, you said the necklace was stolen sometime during the first hour of the party, right?" he asked in a whisper.

Sophia nodded. "But it was probably more like the first half hour. Anyone walking in the hallway by the kitchen would be able to see the schedule, and my mom was supposed to put on the necklace no later than seven forty-five."

Evie nodded. "And the thief wasn't about to get caught red-handed in case she went upstairs early." She looked around the room curiously, her eyes narrowing. "So who was here in the first half hour of the party?"

Sophia pointed to a man in a brown suit who stood huddled behind a cocktail table that had been shoved in the corner. "Arturo Gonzales was the first to arrive. He's the curator of the Minneapolis History

Museum." The man's thinning brown hair was combed over a gleaming bald spot, and he dabbed repeatedly at his forehead with a limp and crumpled handkerchief. His brown-and-tan-striped tie had been loosened, and the top button of his shirt was undone. A half-empty cocktail glass sat on the table in front of him, the beads of condensation on the outside forming a growing wet patch on the white tablecloth.

"Next was Gwendolyn Fairbanks, former diva of the Metropolitan Opera." She nodded her head in the direction of the piano, where the tall woman imperiously waved a gloved hand in the direction of someone seated on the piano bench. The diva smoothed the front of her burgundy velvet gown as opening chords of a melody sounded, and her rich contralto voice filled the room, causing the other guests to look up in surprise. "*Diva* is just the right word, don't you think?" Sophia murmured softly. Evie grinned.

"That's Gideon Doheny and his fiancée, Abigail Morris. He's a venture capitalist." Sophia caught the quizzical looks on the other faces. "He invests money in other people's companies." The others nodded. "Abigail is a kindergarten teacher and an animal lover. She also fosters dogs."

"Cute!" Evie said. "I've always wanted to do that, but my mom won't let me." She felt sorry for Abigail, who looked uncomfortable standing next to her fiancé and his friends. Her sandy-brown hair was cut simply, shoulder-length with bangs. She wore a sleeveless black dress with ballet flats. Her athletic build, late-summer tan, and mosquito bites on her legs showed someone who was more comfortable outside than at a fancy party. She wore no other jewelry than the massive engagement ring on her left hand, which she twisted nervously, her brown doe eyes watching the faces of the other partygoers.

Gideon was telling a boisterous story to a group of people, a glass of champagne in his hand. Occasionally he would punctuate a line with a sweeping gesture, and a dribble of champagne would slop over the rim of the glass. His voice was the loudest in the room. Zach recognized him as the pink-shirted man he had seen in the window earlier. The one with the fake-sounding laugh.

Gwendolyn's aria ended, and she took a deep curtsy. There was a scattering of half-hearted applause in the room, until Gwendolyn's glare urged a more robust response from her captive audience. From the other side of the room a wolf whistle split the air. "That's right, viewers. I'm bringing opera diva Gwendolyn Fairbanks to you live! Don't forget to subscribe to my channel for other surprise concerts, pranks, and celebrity appearances!"

Evie craned her neck to see better, her eyes shining. "Oh, my gosh! That's Jasmine Jetani! She has, like, the nineteenth-most-popular YouTube channel in the world!"

"That's a weirdly specific number," Zach said. He eyed the rainbow-haired YouTuber in distaste. She had flipped her phone around and was filming herself waving and putting bunny ears behind the heads of the fusty old men standing in front of her. Her pink sequined dress seemed aggressively sparkly against the muted tones of the room. "Ugh. What do people see in her? She's so . . . pointless."

Evie folded her arms. "Really? And this is coming from someone whose favorite YouTube channel is some guy talking while he's playing a video game. Talk about pointless!"

"Hey, at least those videos are funny!" Zach said defensively. He nudged his friend. "Back me up, here, Vish."

"You're on your own for this one, dude. I learned a long time ago never to get in the middle of a Mamuya throwdown." Vishal watched the party guests. Some paced like caged animals. Others sat slumped in their chairs, tapping at their smartphones or staring blankly into space. Did one of these people have something to hide? "Were there any other guests here early?"

"None that I can remember, other than a few flocks of old people. They stuck together, though, and they all seem way too frail to be jewel thieves. Some of them barely seem to know what day it is!"

Zach laughed. "So, the folks in this room are our only suspects?"

"You mean other than Evan Masterson?" Sophia challenged.

"Sure, yeah. Other than him."

Sophia nodded. "Those are our suspects."

CHAPTER
7

Vishal nodded his head in the direction of the man in the brown suit. "He looks way too nervous. Let's start with him."

Sophia led the others over to the corner. The group noticed the guests' looks of surprise as they crossed the silk patterned carpet. Sophia smiled graciously, completely in her element. Zach tried to capture her easy confidence. He stood up straighter and squared his shoulders. *Nobody better mistake me for the valet*, he thought. Evie met the other guests' eyes coolly, forcing herself not to try to smooth her ruined braids. Vishal simply grinned and gave a cocky salute when any guest's eyes lingered too long on the disheveled group.

When they reached the cocktail table, they found

Arturo Gonzales poking listlessly at his lukewarm cocktail, his eyes darting back and forth. Tiny beads of sweat clung to his wispy mustache.

"You look a little warm," Sophia said. "Can I offer you something cooler to drink? Some iced water?" Sophia's voice startled Arturo out of his uneasy reverie, and he took an unconscious step away from her, almost as though he were trying to keep the tall table between them.

"No!" he said curtly. "Thank you, but it's been a very long night and I'd just like to go home. Quite frankly, this whole evening has been simply a disaster."

A look of hurt flashed across Sophia's face, and the curator's brittle tone softened somewhat. "Of course, it's far worse for you and your family, I imagine. It must be awful to lose such a precious heirloom." He looked down at his hands. "Such a piece of history . . ." he said wistfully.

Zach nodded his head in an exaggerated expression of woe. "Why would anyone do such a thing?"

"Why indeed!" Arturo said bitterly. "If there's one thing I've learned in my business, it's how many selfish people there are in the world. People who want to keep precious artifacts locked away for themselves, instead of sharing them with the world." His hands tightened into fists. "The North Star necklace is a precious piece of history. It doesn't belong in a safe. It *belongs* in a *museum!*"

"How did you know it was kept in a safe?" Zach asked suspiciously.

The curator rolled his eyes. "The North Star's primary stone is twenty-seven carats. A similar diamond sold at Sotheby's for two-point-five million dollars last year. Only an idiot wouldn't keep it in a safe."

Vishal whistled. "Two-and-a-half million dollars. That's a lot of money. I wouldn't have guessed the Minneapolis History Museum had that kind of money to bid."

Arturo looked away. "Of course we do," he said stiffly. "Our museum has a world-class collection." His eyes blazed. *"World. Class."*

Evie noticed the smirk on Vishal's face and put her hand on his arm, stopping him just before he made a quip that would send the curator completely over the edge. She smiled. "Oh, yeah. Definitely. We went there on a field trip last year, and we were all so impressed with . . . you know, everything, really. Such great stuff. Well done."

Arturo relaxed. "Well, I'm glad at least *someone* thinks so," he said grudgingly. "Honestly, you have no idea how difficult it is to keep a collection fresh and relevant, especially with these new budget cuts."

Sophia's eyes narrowed. "Budget cuts? And how did those impact your bid?"

Arturo shifted uncomfortably. "Well, it could make things a bit of a challenge were the auction to go ahead as planned." He forced a smile. "But I'm confident I could have secured the extra funds."

"Well, it looks like you won't have to worry about that now that the necklace is missing," Zach said pointedly.

The curator drew himself up to his full five-foot-seven-inch height. "I don't know what you think you're implying, young man, but I am certainly not responsible for this evening's misfortune! I haven't left this room the entire night!"

Evie folded her arms. "You're lying."

CHAPTER 8

Evie pointed at the curator's shoes, which were caked in mud. Mud spattered the trousers of his brown suit.

"This . . . this is nothing!" the curator sputtered. "I stumbled on the sidewalk and stepped into a mud puddle on my way into the party."

Sophia pounced. "Nice try, but I saw you talking to my dad at seven fifteen; there wasn't a speck of mud on you then. And I'm sure the police will have no trouble matching your shoes to the muddy prints we found underneath the window!" She raised one pale arm to call over the uniformed sergeant in the doorway.

"Wait!" Arturo cried.

Sophia dropped her hand and looked at him expectantly. "Well?"

The curator closed his eyes for a moment, as though

he were struggling to recollect the evening's events. "I just remembered. I think it's possible that I may have left the room for a . . . short while." He walked over to the open French doors and gestured for the others to follow him outside.

Evie raised her eyebrows. "This should be interesting."

Arturo led them to a quiet corner of the patio, twisting his damp handkerchief in his hands. "I overheard some other party guests talking about their bids. They were much higher than I expected. Much higher." He shook his head.

"So what did you do?" Zach asked.

Arturo gestured to the garden. "I . . . took a breath of fresh air." He looked at the others beseechingly. "You have to understand that the museum had been well positioned to offer a fair-market bid for the North Star. But on the way here I received a call. The board cut my bidding authorization in half. In half! What was I supposed to do? Let the museum become a laughing-stock? They were forcing my hand, pushing me to do something rash."

"Are you confessing to stealing the North Star?" Vishal asked.

Arturo looked alarmed. "Steal it? My goodness, no! How on earth would a reputable museum display a stolen necklace?"

Vishal reddened. "Well, you did say 'something rash,'" he said.

"I meant rash as in resigning from my post, you nitwit. The museum's budget cuts have been increasingly intolerable, but tonight was the last straw. Do you know they cut my salary by twenty percent last year? Twenty percent! And I just took it, because I believed the board was doing what was best for the museum."

Vishal shook his head. "Dude, none of this is making you sound any less guilty."

"You can think what you want," the curator snapped. "When I heard the other potential bids, I knew there was no way we could compete. It's obvious that the board cares more about their own bottom line than the reputation of the museum. So I stepped outside of the party where it was quiet and dictated my letter of resignation into my phone." He slipped his phone out of his pocket and tapped at the screen before handing it to Sophia. "Here. See for yourself."

Sophia saw the date of the voice memo, recorded at 7:40 p.m. She tapped the Play button. *"Ladies and gentlemen of the board, it is with great regret that I must tender my resignation, effective immediately . . ."* She handed the phone back.

"Wait a minute," Evie said. "That still doesn't explain the mud."

A guilty expression passed across Arturo's face. He led them across the patio to a covered veranda. "I had a . . . slight mishap. I was here on the piazza—"

"You mean the porch?" Vishal asked.

"The *piazza*," the curator repeated firmly, "but it was too noisy, so I rounded the corner of the house to find someplace quieter, where I wouldn't be disturbed. I had just found a quiet corner. It was perfect except for this eyesore of a pot. Honestly, it had no business being there; it was absolutely the wrong place for it."

The group followed Arturo around the side of the house until they were standing exactly under the window where they had found the broken pot.

"So the pot was already here," Evie said.

"*I* certainly wouldn't have put it here! Look at it! No concern at all for aesthetics or safety, for that matter. I mean, it was clearly a hazard."

"Why do you say that?" Zach asked.

"I almost broke my neck on this hideous thing! I was deep in thought, working on my letter, when I heard a bloodcurdling scream almost directly above my head." He pointed at the window above. "I was so startled that I stumbled and tripped over it, getting mud all over my favorite suit. And these shoes are obviously a total loss."

"So *you* broke the pot," Sophia said.

The curator drew himself up to his full height. "Hardly," he said huffily. "There's no reason that pot should have been there at all. It was in my way. Honestly, you should count yourself lucky I don't sue!"

Sophia's eyes flashed. "We only have your word that you didn't move the pot yourself."

Zach pointed at something on the ground. "Not just his word. The evidence backs it up."

CHAPTER
9

The group was disappointed to discover that Arturo's footsteps went in the opposite direction from the drag marks of the pot. They followed the officious curator back inside, tired and dispirited.

"Well, that bites. I thought we had this one in the bag. He seemed like the perfect culprit," Vishal said. "He had motive and opportunity, plus he was kind of annoying."

"Just because someone's annoying it doesn't mean they're a criminal," Zach said. "Besides, how would he have gotten the combination to the safe?"

"Oh, yeah," Vishal said sheepishly. "I kinda forgot about that part."

"Well, that still doesn't rule out Evan Masterson,"

Sophia said firmly. "I know he's got to be behind this somehow. I just have to prove it!"

"Zach! Evie! There you are!" The kids looked up to find Mrs. Mamuya waving to them across the room. She looked tired, and the lines in her face sagged, but her blue eyes carried the familiar sparkle that always came with a good story.

When their mother finally wended her way over to them, Zach and Evie introduced her to Sophia. The reporter's eyebrows raised in recognition, and she reached into her coat pocket for her notebook. Evie put her hand on her mother's arm. "Not now, Mom, okay? It's been a long night."

Mrs. Mamuya looked at her watch and nodded. "It's after ten. I should get you kids home." She turned to Sophia, taking in her disheveled hair and tired, drawn face. "Sophia, it was lovely to meet you. I wish it were under better circumstances. I'll do everything I can to help the police track down the thief." She reached into the pocket of her blazer and pulled out her card. "And if you happen remember anything and want to talk . . ."

Sophia stared at the card like it was week-old fish. "I don't talk to reporters," she said flatly, and turned away.

***

Later that night, all was quiet at the Mamuya apartment. Mrs. Mamuya had finally gone to bed after typing her notes into her laptop, and before long, the sound of her gentle snores drifted down the hallway.

Evie's door opened a crack. She had on her mom's old Carleton College sweatshirt and a pair of soft navy joggers. Zach popped his head out of the room next door. Evie could just make out the blue-and-white Lynx WNBA Championship tee he always wore to bed.

"Is the coast clear?"

Evie nodded. "I think so." Evie slipped out of her room and padded down the hallway, Zach and Vishal close behind. A moment later, they were standing in the tiny alcove off the living room that Mrs. Mamuya used as a home office. The cork side walls were tacked with old family photos, to-do lists, and business cards. An overflowing inbox sat on one side, and pens and pencils were clustered into two lumpy clay mugs that Evie and Zach had made in summer camp a few years back. The rest of the desk was scattered with books, newspapers, and Post-it notes and scraps of paper with cryptic messages written in Mrs. Mamuya's distinctive, jagged cursive. The wall behind the desk was a painted chalkboard with rows of neatly labeled built-in cubbies below, some bursting at the seams. Evie noticed a roll of glitter tape and a hairbrush in the "Mailing Supplies" cubby. In a place of honor on the right-hand corner of the desk sat a framed photo of Zach and Evie's father smiling proudly in his police sergeant uniform. He had died when Zach and Evie were toddlers.

"Laptop?" Vishal asked.

Evie sighed. "We can't. It's password-protected. We'll just have to look elsewhere for clues."

"What, exactly, are we hoping to find?" Zach asked. "If Mom found out anything useful, she would have gone straight to the police with it anyway, so how is snooping through her stuff going to help anyone?"

"The thief must be one of the party guests, and Mom had a chance to talk to all of them. Maybe one of them let something slip. Something tiny that Mom might not have known was a clue."

"Are you sure we're talking about the same Mom? The one who figured out you snuck an extra lollipop from the dentist's office because your lips were purple instead of blue? Yeah, I doubt we're gonna find anything that slipped past her tonight."

"Look, do you want to get the necklace back or not?" Evie asked, exasperated.

"Obviously I do," Zach shot back. "I just don't think we should be ransacking our *own mother's* desk to do it. It's not like *she* stole anything."

"Fine," Evie said. "Then Vishal can do it."

"What?!" Vishal's face paled. "Why me?"

"Well, Zach doesn't think we should go through our mother's things, and she's not your mother. So you can do it instead."

Zach sighed. "That does not remotely make sense."

"Look, Mom's notes are the only leads we have. We have to at least look."

"Well, I still don't see why we can't just ask her first."

"Because if we *ask* her, she'll say *no*," Evie explained patiently. She carefully lifted up the freshest-looking pile of paper and scanned its contents. "Nope," she mumbled to herself. "This is all about some trial she's covering." She put the papers down where she found them and pulled open a desk drawer.

"Evie, you should definitely stop now," Zach said. "You might mess something up." Evie ignored him. Zach looked at Vishal. "This is a bad idea, right? Help me out."

Vishal took a step backward and held up his hands. "Don't look at me, dude."

Evie slid the drawer closed and turned to the two boys. "You know, it would go a lot faster if you guys helped me."

"Hang on," Vishal said. "I think I might have found her notebook. And it looks like there's a clue inside that can help us."

CHAPTER
10

Early the next morning, Zach poured cereal into three bowls and set them around the table. Mrs. Mamuya bustled through the house in a pair of black pants and a cream silk blouse. Her hair was wrapped in a towel. "Has anyone seen my hairbrush?"

"It's in the mail cubby behind your desk," Evie said automatically. Zach shot her a look, and Evie shrugged.

"Thanks, 'Vie," her mom said. She grabbed the brush and shoved a stack of papers into her work bag along with her laptop. She tried to fit another stack of paper-clipped documents into the bag, but they wouldn't fit. She paused for a moment and scanned the desk. "Was someone at my desk earlier?"

"Yeah," Evie said. "I couldn't find something."

"Oh no! Did you find it?" Mrs. Mamuya zipped up her bag and dropped it and the stack of documents at one end of the dining table.

"Yup. Thanks, Mom."

As their mom disappeared back into her bedroom, Evie smirked at Zach. "See? And I didn't even have to lie."

"For real." Zach shook his head in an expression of mock woe. "Our own mother . . ."

"Will *thank* us when we get the necklace back and give her the story of the year," Evie said confidently. "So, that clue we found: AM something wine cellar something locksmith. Anybody have any new ideas after last night?"

"It's got to mean there was a locksmith in the wine cellar some morning, right?" Vishal asked. "But how would that connect to the necklace?"

"Maybe if the locksmith was alone, he had the time to sneak upstairs from the wine cellar and make a dummy key to the safe," Zach suggested. "We should call Sophia and check."

Vishal pulled his phone out of the pocket of the

hoodie he had been wearing the night before. He swiped at the screen, then tapped it. Nothing happened. He poked at the various unlock buttons, but the phone didn't respond.

"Is your phone dead?" Zach asked.

"No," Vishal said. "It's just not working."

"That's weird." Zach reached out his hand. "Let me see." He fiddled with the phone. "Usually a phone only gets wacky like this if it's been near strong electrical currents or magnetic waves. You didn't put it on a transformer box or something last night, did you?"

Vishal shrugged. "I don't think so. The only thing it's been near all night is this." He pulled out the shiny hockey puck and handed it to Zach.

"Huh. What kind of waves would this thing give out?" Zach put the puck on the table and slid it across the surface. Suddenly, the stack of documents toppled and flew across the table, the paper clips smacking against the puck. "Whoa! What just happened?!"

"Dude! It's got to be a magnet! That's so awesome!" Vishal pulled at the paper clips that were stuck to the magnet. "Man, they're really stuck on there! I've never seen one this powerful before."

Zach laughed and picked it up. "I wonder what else we can do with it. YouTube?"

"Definitely! Where's your phone?"

Evie rapped on the table. "You guys, focus! I thought we were tracking down that wine cellar clue. Maybe we can call all the locksmith companies and see which one went to the Boyd house recently."

"I thought we were just gonna call Sophia. That's like a million times faster than calling a bunch of random locksmiths."

Evie picked up her empty cereal bowl and dropped it in the sink with a clatter. "No way we're calling her. Did you see how rude she was to Mom last night? '*I don't talk to reporters.*' I mean, where does she get off?"

"Who was rude to me last night?" Mrs. Mamuya asked, walking into the kitchen. Her hair had been blow-dried and smoothed, and she had added a light coating of lipstick to her otherwise bare face.

"No one. Just that rich girl Sophia," Evie said.

"Oh, don't blame her; that happens to me all the

time. People nowadays treat every reporter like we're from that awful gossip rag, the *Twin City Tattler*. I swear it's given journalism a bad name."

***

Sophia's mother picked up her phone from the breakfast table and cried out in alarm. "This is outrageous!"

Mr. Boyd peered over her shoulder. "What happened?"

"Apparently the *Twin City Tattler* wrote an article on the theft last night, and it accuses Maurice outright! It's bad enough that the police were hounding him, but for the paper to name him as the perpetrator without a shred of evidence? It's beyond irresponsible; it's libel! Everyone's going to think the poor man's guilty!" She put the phone down in disgust.

"They're not going to arrest Maurice, are they?" Sophia asked.

"Don't worry," Mrs. Boyd said. "The police can't arrest someone without evidence."

Sophia felt a buzz in the leather-lined phone pocket of her pleated wool miniskirt. The number wasn't familiar. "Hello?"

"Hey, Sophia? It's Zach. Evie said we shouldn't call you—"

"Don't tell her that!" Evie's loud whisper could be heard in the background.

"Okay, um, anyway," Zach continued, "we found something in my mom's notes from last night that could be a clue. Did you have a locksmith do some work in the wine cellar? Maybe in the morning?"

"Hang on," Sophia said. She moved the phone away from her face. "Mom? Dad? Was there a locksmith here recently?"

Both parents shook their heads. "Why?" asked Mr. Boyd.

Sophia shrugged. "No reason, I guess." She picked her phone back up and walked into the kitchen, where the chef and a kitchen helper were having breakfast at the sunny table near the window. "We didn't have any locksmith here," Sophia said into the phone.

"Weird," Zach said. "We found a note that said something about a locksmith in the wine cellar in the AM. Are you sure no one was down there?"

"That is weird. I'll go check and call you back."

Sophia opened the door to the dim, cool cellar and flipped on the light. When she was little, it had been one of her favorite hiding spots during hide-and-seek, and more recently she had often spent time down there with her father, listening and learning as he taught her about the new bottles and vintages he was constantly adding to the family's collection.

When Sophia reached the bottom of the stairs, her mouth hung open in shock. Much of the room was in disarray; bottles of whites and reds were all mixed together, and a few hadn't been put away at all. The wine cellar was Mr. Boyd's pride and joy. How could the staff have left it such a mess?

She stormed back up to the kitchen. "Have you seen the wine cellar this morning? It's a mess!"

The chef looked alarmed. "No! Was anything broken?"

"No, but it's all out of order. I know it was a busy party last night, but I can't believe anyone here would leave it in such a state!"

The kitchen helper, Isabel, was a soft-spoken,

petite women with long hair worn in a tightly coiled bun on top of her head. "Maybe it was the lady who was down there."

Sophia's ears perked up. "What lady?"

"I saw a lady from the party go down there last night. At first, I thought she was lost and looking for the bathroom, but she was there a long time."

"What time was this?" Sophia asked.

"It was early, just before Lucy hurt her ankle. Maybe about seven fifteen?"

Sophia's eyes glistened thoughtfully. "Did you see her come back up?"

Isabel shook her head. "Once Lucy twisted her ankle and dropped the tray, we were scrambling, and I forgot about it."

"Thanks, Isabel," Sophia said. She walked back down to the cellar, turning the question over in her mind. *What would a party guest be doing in the wine cellar?* She looked again, confused by the array of bottles. *She had obviously been searching for something. But what?*

Sophia pulled up the party list on her phone and

ran her finger down the column of names before dialing Zach's number. "Your mom's note wasn't about the morning; it was about one of the guests. And I know who it is!"

Guest List

Ashton W. Nelson
Cecilia Ramirez
Anita Zamora
Mason Lockhart
Archibald Swanson
Ting Fei Long
Corazon di Metillo
Shawn G. Aldridge
John Thomas Crowne
Connor V. Jameson

Guest List

Suzanne Richmonde
Glen Masterson
Stacy Treadwell
Abigail Morris
Stephen Grayson
Constance Wright
Alexander Daly
Amber Takanawa
Gregory Atkinson
Cornelia Jenkins

CHAPTER
11

A short time later, the four young detectives met in front of the neat, well-kept bungalow where Abby lived with her parents. The cedar picket fence was lined with hydrangeas, and there were several well-chewed dog toys dotting the path that led to the front porch.

"So you think AM stands for Abigail Morris, not morning?" Evie asked suspiciously. "I thought you were convinced Evan Masterson was the culprit. So what are we doing here?"

"Your mom's notes said something about AM in the wine cellar. A female guest was seen going down there at the party last night, and it looks like she totally ransacked the place. I want to know what she was looking for," Sophia said.

"Oh, so now all of the sudden you think my mom has a worthwhile clue? I thought you don't listen to reporters."

Sophia rolled her eyes. "I said I don't *talk* to them, okay? So, cool your jets, Evie. It's nothing personal."

Evie put her hands on her hips. "Well, it sure feels personal. What do you have against reporters, anyway?"

Sophia leveled her gaze at Evie. "Look. Between my dad's business deals and my mom's cases, my family's kind of in the paper a lot, okay? It hasn't done us any favors, so I'm not suddenly gonna start chatting with a reporter like some dumb noob; I don't care who it is."

"Well, you didn't have to be so rude about it."

Sophia opened the gate and walked into the yard. "Take it from me. Sometimes being rude is the only way to get people to listen."

The boys hesitantly trailed after Sophia up to the porch, and after a moment, Evie followed. Sophia rang the bell, and a there was a deep bark from inside. Clicking claws galloped through the house.

When Abigail Morris opened the door, three dogs squeezed around her and strained their necks to sniff at the visitors. "Sophia Boyd!" Abby said with shock. "This is a surprise! Who are your friends?"

The kids introduced themselves, and Abby invited them inside. As soon as they sat down, the largest dog, a black-and-white pit bull mix, shoved a well-chewed stuffed alligator into Evie's hand. "That's Ronin," Abby said. "She loves to play fetch." Evie tossed the toy, and the big dog pounced on it before bringing it back to her for another round.

A small, three-legged dog with a feathery white tail hopped onto the sofa next to Zach. She immediately flopped onto her side and looked up hopefully. "That's Thumbelina Feathertail," Abby said. "She's always asking for belly rubs." Zach grinned and petted the dog's pink tummy.

Vishal pointed to the tiny tan-and-white fluffball standing in the middle of the living room. Her round eyes were milky, and a pink tongue lolled out of her toothless mouth. "Is that dog okay?"

Abby chuckled. "She's fine. Chicken is mostly deaf and blind, so she's just trying to figure out where everyone is." Abby clapped her hands loudly, and the little dog perked up and trotted over to her feet. The young woman scooped her into her arms, and Chicken immediately curled up in her lap. "So, what can I do for you guys?"

Sophia folded her arms. "Well, I'd like to know what you were doing in my wine cellar last night."

Abby blinked. "Oh."

Sophia pressed on. "You don't deny you were down there?"

Abby shook her head. "Of course not. I *offered* to go."

"So you were working for someone else. I knew it! Was it Evan Masterson?"

Abby looked puzzled. "Is that your caterer?"

"What?"

Zach held up his hands. "Hold up a second. Can everyone please just slow down?" Zach looked at Abby. "Let's start over. You said you offered to go down to the wine cellar. Why?"

Abby stroked Chicken's head. "Gideon's wonderful, and it's been a whirlwind since we've gotten engaged. He's always whisking me off to glamorous parties . . ." She looked down at the sparkling diamond engagement ring on her hand. ". . . but sometimes it's a bit lonely at those things. Everyone's so different from the kind of people I grew up with."

"Different how?" Vishal asked, curious.

"My parents didn't have a lot of money for college, so I used to help out with a catering company on evenings and weekends to put myself through school. It was nothing fancy, just passing out trays of food, but I loved it. Everyone helping each other out, cracking jokes."

Evie grinned. "My mom's first high school job was working as a deli waitress. She said the same thing."

Abby smiled back at her. "Last night, Gideon had to take a phone call, and I got a little tired of standing around and making small talk with a bunch of people I didn't know. I recognized one of the servers from my catering days, so I popped into the kitchen to see if she needed any help."

Evie's eyes widened. "You did? OMG! What did she say?"

Abby blushed again and grinned. "She said, 'Thank goodness you're here,' and sent me straight to the cellar to bring up more white wine!"

Evie laughed, but Sophia glowered. "A likely story! I saw the cellar this morning, and the place was completely ransacked. What were you looking for?"

Abby shrugged. "Wine," she replied simply. "Nobody in my family drinks. The only way I can tell a white from a red is from the color inside the bottles. It was so dark in the cellar I couldn't see the difference, so I had to keep grabbing bottles and running over to hold them up to the light. Then I couldn't remember where to put them back."

"Nice try. But you already said you worked for a catering company." Sophia smirked and cocked her head to one side. "Those places always serve wine. Are you really trying to tell us you never learned the difference between a Merlot and a Chardonnay?"

Chicken stretched her neck up and yawned, and Abby scratched her under the chin. "Like I said, I mostly just brought out food," continued Abby. "When I did serve wine, I just had to ask if they wanted red or white and hand them a glass someone else had already poured. It's a good thing I don't have to serve at my own wedding; I'd be useless!"

Sophia folded her arms and didn't say anything.

"When are you and Gideon getting married?" Evie asked.

"Next August," Abby answered. "I teach kindergarten, and trying to plan a wedding during the school year would be a nightmare. Especially with the kind of wedding Gideon wants. He has a huge heart, and he's so generous, but it's all a bit much for me. At one point, he was talking about hiring live tigers to be the ring bearers!"

"That sounds . . . dangerous," Vishal said.

Abby laughed. "That's Gideon. Ever the showman. He always says, 'If you can't do it big, it's not worth doing.'"

"Some people are saying that it's going to be the most lavish wedding Minneapolis has ever seen," Sophia said, eyeing Abby carefully.

Abby shrugged. "That's Gideon."

Sophia narrowed her eyes. "Something's not adding up."

CHAPTER
12

Sophia pointed to the article in the wedding magazine. "If Gideon's planning a huge, expensive wedding in Minneapolis, then what are you doing reading articles about planning weddings on a budget?"

Abby sighed. "I'm worried," she finally admitted. She cuddled Chicken closer. "Lately Gideon hasn't been himself. He seems nervous. On edge. I've heard him arguing on the phone with his business partner. I think he might be having money problems, but he says that everything's fine." She twisted her engagement ring around her finger.

"If Gideon's having money problems, then why would he want to bid on the North Star?" Zach asked.

"I don't know," Abby said. "Gideon always says he wants me to have the best of everything, but I don't even like jewelry."

"Or maybe you stole the North Star to help Gideon out of his money problems," Sophia said accusingly. "Were you working alone, or did someone hire you? Was it Evan Masterson?"

Evie threw up her hands in exasperation. "OMG, relax about Evan Masterson for a hot second, will you?"

Sophia ignored her. "If you stole the necklace, you would never have to worry about money problems again. No more slaving away at your dead-end job, living in this tiny shack with your parents." She gestured around the cozy, well-appointed living room.

Abby bristled. "I live here with my parents because I *choose* to, and I'm proud of my job. I teach children to read. Do you know how amazing that is? I would never steal. Never in a million years!"

Evie's jaw dropped. "Seriously, Sophia, do you have any idea how to treat people at all?"

Sophia brushed the jab away dismissively. "Well, what about the whole locksmith thing?" she demanded.

"What exactly is the locksmith thing?" Vishal asked. "I thought she was a kindergarten teacher."

"My dad was a locksmith," Abby explained, "but he's retired."

"And only a locksmith—or possibly a locksmith's daughter—would be able to open the safe without the combination," Sophia said.

"Well, not necessarily," Abby said.

Sophia was triumphant. "See? I told you she knows something!"

"Wait, what did you mean by 'not necessarily'?" Vishal asked Abby. "How could someone who's not an expert safecracker get into a safe?"

"It depends on what kind it is," Abby said, setting down Chicken. "Let me go get my dad. He can explain."

As soon as she left the room, Evie turned on Sophia. "Sophia, for real. You can't just go around accusing everyone. And what's with that burn about her house and her job?"

Vishal reached down for Chicken and pulled her into his lap. "Yeah, Sophia, that was mad abrasive."

"Yeah, well, when you have a multimillion dollar

heirloom stolen from your home, then you can lecture me on how polite I should be," Sophia shot back resentfully.

Abby returned with her father, Mr. Morris. He was a short but solidly built man with white hair and light-blue eyes set wide apart on his face. "Well, hello there, kids. Abby here says you have a question about safecracking. You aren't planning any heists, now, are you?" he joked, his voice betraying the long, flat vowels of a native Minnesotan.

Sophia's expression was icy, and as she opened her mouth to speak, Zach interjected. "Actually, sir, the crime has already happened. We're trying to figure out how someone could open a safe without the combination or any sign that it's been broken into."

Abby's father rubbed his hands together. "Now, that's an interesting puzzle. Do you know what kind of safe it is?"

"I know what it looks like, but I don't know what kind it is," Sophia said.

"Why don't you all follow me back to my workshop, and we'll see what we can figure out." The old man led Abby and the kids through the back door and into a small detached garage. The inside had been converted into an office with a workbench and old safes in varying states of disassembly. Dozens of lockpicks and keys hung on hooks along a pegboard wall, and an old-fashioned phone the color of Band-Aids sat in the corner of the beat-up metal desk near the door.

Mr. Morris picked up a thick white binder from the desk and flipped it open. "Why don't you thumb through this book to see if anything looks familiar?"

"Cool," Vishal said. "It's like a police lineup, only for safes!"

Sophia bent over the book, tucking her hair behind her ear. After a few moments, she pointed to a photograph of a large black safe with an electronic keypad. "I'm pretty sure that's it."

As the group bent over to read over the safe's specs, Zach nudged Vishal with an excited grunt. "Vish! Look!"

CHAPTER 13

Vishal groaned. "Oh, man! That magnet we found in the garden . . ."

"That's what the thief must have used to break into the safe," Zach finished.

"We have to bring it to the police!" Evie slumped. "But I guess any hope for fingerprints is out."

Sophia and the adults exchanged confused glances. Evie and the boys explained what they had found in the garden.

"And you knuckleheads picked it up, *played with it*, and didn't even think to tell the police?" Sophia demanded.

"It looked like a hockey puck," Vishal said defensively. "How were we supposed to know it was a clue?"

"Oh, I don't know, maybe the fact that you were at a *crime scene*?" Sophia shot back.

"Where is the magnet now?" asked Abby's father.

"It's in my backpack," Vishal said sheepishly. He slung the pack off his back and started to unzip it.

"Don't touch it again," Abby said. "There's always a possibility there could be something the police could still use. I'll be right back."

She returned a few minutes later with a pair of rubber gloves and a resealable plastic bag. Mr. Morris put on the gloves and placed the magnet carefully into the bag, sealing it tight. Vishal reached for the bag, but Sophia blocked his hand. "*I'll* carry that. You've done enough damage, don't you think?" Vishal's ears turned pink and he dropped his hand.

Evie flashed her brightest smile at Abby and her father. "Would one of you mind giving us a ride to the police station?"

***

A short time later, the four teens sat on a hard wooden bench in the police station lobby as a stone-faced uniformed officer stared them down over the top of the counter. "Let me get this straight: you four children claim to have discovered evidence that is . . ." He looked down at the pink message pad on the desk, his voice laced with amused disbelief. ". . . of importance to the North Star case."

"Of *vital* importance," Sophia corrected. She pointed at his pad. "Vital. Write that down."

The officer's dark, bushy eyebrows crawled up his forehead as he gazed at her over the top of his reading glasses. He looked down at his message pad. "Of *vital* importance to the case." He made a big show of writing in the missing word. Then he put down his pen and smiled politely. "All right, then. Have a seat." He turned back to a handwritten report he was painstakingly transcribing into an ancient desktop computer. All that could be heard was the clacking of his keyboard and the distant ringing of phones in the offices beyond.

Sophia watched him for a moment. "Well?" she said finally. "Aren't you going to tell someone? The police chief, maybe? I'm sure they'll want to see us right away."

The officer's eyes never left the computer screen. "Mm-hm. The police chief oversees the entire force, but she's always ready to drop everything for a crime tip from a couple of kids."

Sophia smiled confidently. "Great!" The officer at the desk didn't move. Sophia leaned over to Evie, her voice a piercing whisper. "He's not doing anything. Do you think maybe he's being sarcastic?"

Evie closed her eyes for a moment. "He's definitely being sarcastic," she replied in a low voice.

"So what do we do, then?"

Evie summoned from the depths of her rapidly depleting well of patience. "We wait, Sophia."

Sophia blinked. "But this is important! Why should we have to wait?"

Evie slouched back against the bench and stretched her legs out in front of her. "Because that's what regular people do. Maybe if you're rich and white, folks jump up at the snap of your fingers. I wouldn't know. But whenever the rest of us asks for something, someone else tells us to sit down and wait our turn. And if we're lucky—*if we're lucky*—then maybe eventually someone will show up and listen to us. But more often than not, they won't."

"But that's not fair!" Sophia protested.

Evie locked eyes with Sophia. "Believe me, we know."

Sophia looked at the two boys. They nodded and shrugged. "Oh," Sophia said in a small voice. "Okay." She placed the bagged magnet in her lap and folded her hands neatly on top of it.

After what felt like hours, the officer at the front desk finished typing up his report and shut the manila folder with a sigh. He stood up and stretched, his protruding belly straining against the buttons of his dark-blue uniform. He picked up the message pad and glanced at it again. "I'll drop this off on my way to the can. Don't touch anything while I'm gone."

Vishal grimaced and jumped up from the bench. "I hate it when they say that. It makes me want to touch everything!" He paced around the waiting area.

"I know, right?" Zach stood up and riffled through a display of brochures on a side table.

"What's 'the can'?" Sophia asked. "Is it some cop thing?"

Evie looked sideways at Sophia. "It's the bathroom."

"Oh!" Sophia wrinkled her nose. "Gross. That is serious TMI."

Evie giggled in spite of herself. "Tell me about it!"

Just then, a plainclothes police officer stepped into the lobby from the back, his eyes intent on the screen of the cell phone he held in his hand. He had dark hair and coppery skin, and his gray suit stretched across his broad shoulders. He looked up in surprise when he saw the group of young teens wandering around the waiting room. "What are you doing here? Are you waiting for someone?"

Zach put down the brochure he had been reading. "We are, actually." He held out his hand. "I'm Zach Mamuya, and this is my sister, Evie—"

The officer stopped him. "Did you say Mamuya? You're not Yaro's twins, are you?" Zach nodded, and the officer's face broke out in a grin. "I can't believe how grown you are! I still remember how excited he was when you two were born. You were all he talked about!" The man shook Zach's hand and offered his hand to Evie. "I'm Detective Peter Bermudez. Your dad trained me back when I was a rookie cop just learning the ropes. It was an honor to serve under him."

Zach and Evie introduced their friends, and the detective looked at them expectantly. "I was just headed out for lunch, but is there something I can help with?"

"Well, we found a clue that we think is related to the North Star theft, but we can't get anyone to listen to us. Would you take a look at it?"

"I'm one of the detectives assigned to the North Star case." He glanced at his watch. "Lunch can wait. Why don't you come back to my desk?"

He led them to a cramped cubby with a bland laminate desk and two overstuffed filing cabinets. One wall of the cubby was corkboard, with labeled photos and diagrams tacked to it. In the center was a close-up photo of the North Star. "Whoa!" Vishal pointed at the board with awe. "It's just like on TV! Where's all the red string you use to connect everything?"

Detective Bermudez chuckled. "Sorry to disappoint you, but we don't do the string thing here. But the boards are great; it's really helpful to see everything in one place. Now why don't you tell me about this clue you found?"

The group filled the detective in on their adventures thus far, from the spy in the hedges to their visit to the Morris house. They handed over the bagged magnet.

"It's too bad about the fingerprints," the detective said. "But we may still be able to find something."

"I have one question," Zach said. "How exactly can a magnet break into a safe?"

Detective Bermudez stood up. "I'll show you." The kids followed him to a conference room with a long table at one end and a half-erased whiteboard pushed against the wall. In one corner stood a black metal safe with an electronic keypad. "This safe is the same model as the one found in the Boyds' dressing room." He looked at Sophia. "Look about right to you?"

Sophia nodded.

He held up the magnet, still in its resealable bag. "Ready to see a magic trick?" He gestured to Evie. "Evie, go see if you can open the safe."

Evie pulled at the handle. "It's locked."

The detective nodded. "Watch this." He slipped the bagged magnet into a sock and ran it over the front of the safe near the handle. "The sock makes it easier to move the magnet around." He bent his head close to the front of the safe.

"What are you listening for?" Vishal asked.

"The solenoid. That's what activates the locking mechanism, and it's usually made of nickel. A rare-earth magnet like this is powerful enough to move the solenoid, even through the heavy door." He slowly slid the sock near the door handle, and a few seconds later, there was a click. "Voilà!" The detective turned the handle and opened the safe. "Locksmiths have been using this little trick for years."

"Locksmiths," Sophia said. "So does that mean Abby is the prime suspect?" She turned to Evie. "See? I was right to question her!"

Detective Bermudez held up one hand. "It's too soon to jump to any conclusions. Anyone could go on YouTube and find videos of exactly what I showed you. And it sounds like Ms. Morris was more than gracious when it came to helping you with your questions. She even gave you a ride to the police station. That's not typical behavior for a guilty party."

"So you're basically saying anyone could have done it?" Sophia asked with a weary sigh.

"Not just anyone. The thief would need knowledge, motive, and opportunity," the detective said, ticking the words off on his fingers. He looked at his watch again. "Now, if you'll excuse me, I need to log this into evidence before a meeting with my captain. I'll have another officer escort you out."

As they walked back to the policeman's cubby, Evie looked around at the rabbit warren of desks and cubbies. "I was just wondering. Which desk was my dad's?"

Detective Bermudez smiled sadly. "The precinct house underwent a big renovation about eight years ago, so everything was different from when he was here. But his name is on the wall outside the captain's office."

He walked them over to wooden plaque that said, *Remembering the Fallen.* Beneath were brass plates with names and dates. Evie recognized her father's name: *Yaro Mamuya,* and the year he died. Evie found herself reaching for her brother's hand. They had been three, so they remembered little about him. All they had left of him now were their mother's stories and the birthday cards sent from their grandparents in Tanzania.

The policeman put his hands on the twins' shoulders. "Your father was good police and a good man. He never stopped pushing us to be the best cops we could be." After a moment, the group continued down the hallway.

Back in the detective's cubby, his desk phone rang. "Bermudez," he said shortly into the phone. He picked up a pad and pen and started taking notes. "Uh-huh . . . yeah . . . go on . . ." With his free hand, he dug into a drawer, searching for a manila envelope.

While he was distracted, the kids took a closer look at the North Star crime board. There were photos of the party, the dressing room, and the guests. In one photo, a group of party guests stood smiling in front of the grand staircase. Zach leaned closer and pointed. "Is that what I think it is?"

CHAPTER
14

"That's Gideon Doheny walking upstairs," Evie said under her breath. "And what's he holding in his hand?"

"It looks like the magnet," Sophia answered. She turned to Detective Bermudez, who had just hung up the phone. "Has Doheny been questioned? Why isn't he under arrest?"

The detective gently shepherded the group out of his cubby and back toward the lobby. "We are pursuing all possible avenues. I'm not allowed to share my list of suspects with you, but you have to trust us. And it's important that you take a step back and let us do our job." He reached into his pocket and pulled out a business card. "Here's my card if you ever need something again."

"But we can help," Vishal said. "Just look at how we found the magnet. That was an important clue!"

Detective Bermudez looked pained. "I'm really glad you brought it to us, but if you hadn't picked it up and taken it with you last night, we could have found it a lot sooner." He stopped at the front door. "Listen, you're great kids, and I appreciate all that you've done to try to help, but chasing criminals is dangerous work. It's time to leave the policing to the professionals, okay?"

"Got it," Vishal said, and the others nodded in reluctant agreement.

The kids walked to the bus stop where they parted ways, their faces glum. "See you at school tomorrow," Zach said to Sophia. "Do you want to sit with us at lunch? I know you're still new, so we can introduce you to some of our other friends. It's a pretty good crew."

A black SUV with tinted windows pulled up to the bus stop. Sophia opened the back door. "No thanks. I have enough friends," she tossed over her shoulder, and climbed into the car.

***

The next day at school, Zach, Evie, and Vishal passed

alking alone in the hall. Zach waved, but
oked right through them. Evie hit Zach's arm.
..., ..d you wave? She obviously doesn't want to be
friends with us."

Vishal ran his fingers through his spiky hair. "Oh,
don't be so hard on her, Evie. She likes us; she's just
prickly."

"Why do you keep making excuses for her?" Evie
demanded. "Is it because she's pretty?"

Vishal and Zach looked at each other. "Honestly,
no," Vishal said. "I guess I feel kind of bad for her.
Don't you?"

"Why would I feel bad for a spoiled white girl who
treats everybody like dirt?" Evie asked, incredulous.
"Seriously, if we acted the way she did, nobody would
be feeling sorry for us."

Zach shrugged. "I don't know; I just do. She doesn't
really seem to have any friends."

Evie exploded. "Of course she doesn't have any
friends! Look at the way she talks to people!"

"Fine," Zach said. "You don't have to be friends with
her. But I'm going to keep trying."

***

That afternoon, Zach, Evie, and Vishal arrived at the flagpole, their usual meeting place after school, at almost the same time. "My house today?" Vishal asked. "I can probably convince my mom to make samosas."

"Yum! I'm in," Evie said.

"There's no time for samosas," a voice drawled behind them. "We need to find out what Gideon Doheny was doing on that staircase."

Evie turned around to find Sophia standing there, phone in hand. "I've already ordered a car."

"I guess you'll be in it alone, then, because we already have plans," Evie said.

"Considering I heard you make the plans about thirty seconds ago, I doubt they're set in stone," Sophia said.

"Yeah, well, the world doesn't revolve around you," Evie retorted. "You can't just order us around and expect us to do it." She turned to the two boys. "Right, guys?"

Vishal shifted his feet and shrugged. "I don't know, Evie. I mean, after that photo yesterday, don't you want to hear what Doheny has to say? It's not like the cops are going to tell us anything."

"Exactly!" Sophia said. "I knew you guys would get it. Let's go." She started walking to the corner.

Zach held up a hand. "Hold a beat, Sophia." He turned to Evie. "You don't have to go."

Evie folded her arms. "I'm waiting for the 'but' . . ."

Zach sighed. "But I really want to." Seeing the look on Evie's face, he hurried on. "Look, we're tracking down a thief! That's pretty hard to say no to." He nudged her. "Don't tell me you aren't having fun."

"It's not about whether it's fun. It's the principle of the thing. The girl wouldn't even wave to you today."

Zach put his hands in his pockets. "You're right. That was messed up. But maybe we can give her one more chance."

Evie bit her lip, thinking. Finally, she said, "Fine. One more chance. But only because I'm interested in the case, not because Sophia asked us." As she followed Zach to the car, her step quickened. "I can't wait to hear what Doheny has to say for himself!"

***

Gideon Doheny's office was in a tall glass building downtown. The lobby was a gleaming expanse of marble and chrome, and the polished elevator doors closed noiselessly as the teens pushed the button for the top floor.

When the elevator doors opened, the group walked into an office in disarray. Huge pieces of art leaned against the empty walls, and workers in coveralls knelt over one of the paintings, wrapping it in moving blankets and thick brown paper.

The doors were all open and the reception desk was empty, so the group followed the sound of raised voices until they found Gideon's corner office. Gideon stood behind a sleek, glass-topped desk that was awash with papers and files, shouting into a speakerphone and running his hands frantically through his immaculately cut dark hair. His silk tie was loosened around the collar, and there were dark circles under his eyes. He and the person at the other end of the line were shouting over each other so much that the kids couldn't hear what either party was saying. Finally, Gideon screamed, "Fine! I'll see you in court!" and hung up the phone in a rage. It was then that he looked up and noticed the group of kids watching him from the doorway. No one said anything for a moment.

"Is this a bad time?" Sophia asked sweetly.

Her question seemed to shock Gideon into action. He quickly smoothed his hair, straightened his tie, and flashed them one of his signature megawatt smiles. "Of course not! It's just another day in this business." He gestured at the half-full cardboard boxes that scattered the floor. "Sorry about the mess. We're doing some redecorating."

Evie shot her brother the side-eye. This didn't look like any redecorating she had ever seen.

"What can I do for you kids?" Gideon asked.

"We have a few questions for you," Sophia said.

"Ah, school project? I've got a busy afternoon, but I can certainly spare a few moments for the younger generation. After all, you guys are the future, right?" He chuckled at the cliché, as though he had said something exceptionally clever.

Zach sighed inwardly. "Actually, sir, it's about the North Star. You were planning to bid on it, right?"

Gideon's face arranged itself into an expression of

dismay. "Yes, what a terrible tragedy. I had my heart set on giving it to my fiancée as a wedding gift." He glanced up at Sophia, and his forehead wrinkled with careful concern. "And, of course, what an even deeper loss for your family. You must be heartbroken."

"My biggest heartbreak is for the gibbons at the zoo. Whoever stole that necklace stole their home."

Gideon shook his head in studied sympathy. "Of course. The gibbons, the gibbons. Think of the poor gibbons." He fiddled with a paper clip on his desk and watched the kids out of the corner of his eye.

"So, you were going to bid on the necklace—"

"And help the gibbons," Sophia interjected.

"—and help the gibbons," Vishal continued, "but it disappeared before you had the opportunity to make an offer."

"Unfortunately, yes," Gideon said.

Vishal pushed harder. "How exactly were you planning on buying the necklace when you clearly can't afford it?"

"What are you talking about?!" Gideon blustered. "My firm is one the most successful in the Twin Cities.

I've been on the cover of *Yacht Magazine*, for Pete's sake!" He pointed at a glass-framed photo on the half-empty glass-and-chrome shelves. The magazine cover showed a grinning Gideon wearing a captain's hat and standing on the deck of a huge white boat.

"Oh, please!" Sophia brushed the words away. "Anyone can fake a magazine cover and put it up on a wall." She pointed at the mess of papers in front of him. "Your desk tells a different story."

CHAPTER
15

Sophia reached over and pulled out a yellow paper from one of the stacks on his desk. The words *NOTICE OF EVICTION* were printed across the top in angry red letters. "It says here you're being evicted from the building because you haven't paid rent."

Gideon's shoulders tensed, and his face tightened. "Oh, that's just a misunderstanding," he said. His voice was smooth, but the kids could hear tension behind it. "I have plenty of money. Tons! This is just complicated business stuff; you kids wouldn't understand. In fact, I closed a deal a few months ago, and there will be millions coming in any day now. Maybe even billions!"

Everyone looked at each other. Finally, Evie spoke. "We saw Abby yesterday. She's worried about you."

Gideon's composure crumbled, and the confidence in his voice collapsed into despair. "I promised Abby the moon, and I'm not going to let her down just because of a few risky business investments. It's not fair to her. She deserves nothing but the best!"

"What kind of risky investments?" Zach asked.

Gideon sighed. "It was a means of capturing excess human methane to create electrical power. Great for the environment, a hundred percent sustainable, and totally clean. We even had the perfect tagline: 'The Real Natural Gas!'"

The kids looked at each other. "Let me get this straight," Vishal said slowly. "You invested in a company that was going to turn people's *farts* into fuel?"

Gideon put his head in his hands and moaned. "It was supposed to be the future of energy. I mean, it's perfect, right?"

The kids shifted uncomfortably in their seats. "Uh, yeah . . . sure." Zach tried to put some semblance of confident enthusiasm in his voice, but it fell flat. He carefully avoided looking at the others.

Evie struggled to suppress a smile. Her eyes met

Vishal's, and a frantic giggle burbled out of him. He tried to cover it with a cough. Zach's lips were pressed tightly together. Finally, the three friends could hold it no longer and burst into hysterics. Vishal went as limp as a noodle and slithered out of his chair, his distinctive, high-pitched giggle pushing the twins into even greater convulsions.

Sophia sat stonily in her chair, her back ramrod straight. Finally she let out an exasperated sigh. "Oh, grow up! Honestly, I don't see what's so funny about making fuel from human gas."

Evie clutched her stomach, still breathless from laughing. "Everything, Sophia. Literally everything is funny about that."

Sophia looked sympathetically at Gideon. "Ignore them. They just don't know a good business opportunity when they see one."

Gideon shook his head sadly. "No, they're right. This is exactly what potential investors did during all of our presentations. It was a complete bust."

Vishal climbed back into his chair, still wiping tears of laughter from his eyes. "I'm sorry, Mr. Doheny. That's a total bummer."

"But wait, if that's really the case, then how *were* you planning to pay for the North Star?" Zach asked.

"I would have figured something out," Gideon answered, waving his hand vaguely.

"Something like . . . stealing it?" Evie asked. "We saw a photo that shows you leaving the party and walking upstairs with something in your hand. That would have given you a perfect opportunity to break into the safe and steal the necklace."

"Don't be absurd," Gideon asked impatiently. "I don't even have the combination."

"Oh, come on," Vishal pushed. "Your future father-in-law is a locksmith. Don't tell me you haven't picked up a few things."

"Oh, for Pete's sake," Gideon said. "Do you really think I would risk everything I've built just to give my fiancée a necklace she couldn't even wear? The North Star is the most recognizable piece of jewelry in the Twin Cities. If the thief were seen in public with it even once, then it's game over." He tapped on his phone and peered at the screen. "During the party, I got a call from my business partner, Morris Fareed. Our conversations tend to be fairly heated lately, so I went upstairs to a private room where I wouldn't be overheard." He slapped the phone down and slid it across the desk. "Here. Unless I'm the world's greatest actor, there's no way I could have pulled off a jewel heist."

The kids crowded around the phone. After a few seconds, Zach lifted his head. "He's right."

3:16 PM
Call History

< Contacts

Save

Carter Harrington
September 20
5:29 PM   2 mins

Adelaide Finnegan
September 20
2:01 PM

Morris Fareed
Sepember 19
7:20 PM   25 mins

Trisha Masterson
September 19
8:07 AM

Kyle Harris
September 17
2:49 AM   1 hour 39 mins

Connect   Call Logs   History   Help

chapter 16

Zach pointed at the phone's call log. "You were definitely on the phone with Mr. Fareed during the time of the burglary."

"Unless he's just providing a false alibi?" Evie said suspiciously.

"You're welcome to call him and ask," Gideon said wearily. "He hates my guts at the moment, so you don't have to worry about whether or not he's lying to cover for me. He most certainly wouldn't."

"If money's so tight, I still don't understand why you would want to bid on the necklace in the first place. Your fiancée says she doesn't even like jewelry," Zach said.

"I know." Gideon pushed his swivel chair away from the desk and turned to face the wall of windows behind him, staring at the city skyline. "It's just that I didn't want Abby to know I was having money troubles. What if she found out and then changed her mind about marrying me? I'd be lost without her!"

"I'm pretty sure she already knows about the money," Evie said, "so I think you'd both be a lot happier if you just told her what's going on. My mom always said that when she married my dad, they didn't have two cents to rub together, but she wouldn't have changed a thing." She leaned forward. "Tell Abby the truth, Mr. Doheny. I promise you won't regret it."

***

As the group walked out of the office, they could already hear Gideon weeping into the phone. "My darling lambikins! I'm so sorry I haven't been honest with you!"

Vishal elbowed Zach. *"Lambikins,"* he whispered. Zach grinned. The elevator doors closed behind them.

The kids arrived in the lobby and stepped onto the sidewalk. It was near the end of the workday, and the street was starting to fill up with traffic and pedestrians in business suits. Zach glanced around. "Wow. It sure got busy since we went in."

"Yeah," Vishal said. His eyes searched for the nearest bus stop, and he pointed. "Over there. We can take the 6C bus." The others followed.

"So, if Gideon can't be the thief, then we're right back where we started," Evie said, "with zero suspects."

"Not zero," Sophia retorted. "Don't forget Evan Masterson."

Evie threw up her hands. "For the last time, Sophia, it's obviously not him! You saw for yourself that his footprints didn't match the ones at the crime scene."

"I don't care. Even if he didn't steal it himself, he's got to be involved somehow. Why else was he there?"

"You don't even know it was him that you saw that night," Evie said. When Sophia didn't respond, Evie started walking to the nearest bus stop. "Whatever," she finally mumbled. "You go chase after Evan Masterson if you want to. We're going over to Vishal's for samosas." She looked at the two boys. "Right?"

"Yeah, sure," Vishal said, distracted. He was busy watching the street. After a moment, he held his phone up and flashed a big smile for a selfie.

"Dude. What are you doing?" Zach asked.

Vishal tapped at his phone. "I'm just texting my mom to see if Sophia can come, too." He looked at Sophia. "I mean, if you want to."

Evie scoffed. "Don't bother, Vish. She doesn't want to hang out with us."

Zach put his hand on his sister's shoulder. "Come on, Evie. Don't be like that."

"Like what? Realistic? Sophia only shows up when she wants something, and then when she's done with us, she goes back into her shiny black car to her perfect life. Anyone can see that she's just using us."

Sophia bristled. "That's not true! I'm not using you!"

Evie crossed her arms. "Okay. Fine. Then come to Vishal's with us." The bus pulled up to the stop behind her and the doors opened with a hiss. A small group of people spilled out of the front door.

An elderly lady with a cane shuffled carefully down

the steps, gripping the handrail tightly. Vishal held out his arm at the bottom of the steps, and the woman reached for his shoulder gratefully until her cane found surer footing on the sidewalk. Vishal and the twins climbed onto the bus and looked back at Sophia expectantly.

"Well?" Evie asked.

Sophia bit her lip and looked at the ground. "I can't. I'm busy."

"That's what I thought," Evie said. The doors closed and the bus pulled away.

***

The three friends slouched in the back of the bus, looking out the window to where Sophia stood on the sidewalk alone. "Man, Evie, that was cold," Zach said quietly.

"Why?" Evie demanded.

"I don't know. Did you see her face? It looks like she felt really bad."

Evie straightened in her seat. "Why should her feelings be more important than mine? If I don't like the way she treats us, I'm allowed to tell her that."

"Yeah, well, maybe it's not personal. Maybe it's just how she is."

"And maybe this is just how *I* am. I don't think it's wrong to expect someone to be a decent friend."

Zach stretched across Vishal and looked into his sister's eyes. "I'm not saying you're wrong."

"Then what are you saying?"

Zach leaned back and folded his arms, turning his gaze to the window. "I don't know, Evie. Just forget it."

There was a long moment of silence. Vishal cleared his throat. "Yeah, uh, remind me not to sit between you two anymore." His joke broke the tension, and the twins laughed self-consciously.

"Sorry, Vish," Zach said. The three grew quiet again, looking out the back window at the late-afternoon light falling on the street behind them.

After a few stops, the bus turned a corner and Vishal shifter closer to the window. He pulled out his phone and snapped a quick a photo through the back window.

"What is it?" Evie asked.

The bus pulled up to the Uptown Transit Station,

and a large crowd of people stood up and pushed to the front of the bus. Vishal got up, too. "Let's get off here."

"Why?" Zach asked. "This isn't our stop."

"Just follow me, okay? And stay close." Vishal pulled the hood of his sweatshirt over his head and squeezed into the crowd of exiting passengers. He started walking toward the front of the bus, and Evie and Zach followed slowly, nonplussed. He turned to see them hanging back, and reached for Zach's hand. "Stay with the crowd," he hissed, pulling his friends after him.

The station was bustling with activity, and Vishal followed the crowd into the building, never looking back. Zach and Evie followed close behind. Vishal led them down the ramp to the pedestrian path below. "Where are we going?" Evie asked.

Vishal pulled out his phone and showed them the two photos he took. "Somewhere where a car can't follow us."

CHAPTER
17

The next day at lunch, Vishal and the twins sat with their heads bent close together. "I don't know, Vish. I thought about it last night, and even though the black sports car was in both of the photos, I don't know if it was really following us," Zach said. "Maybe the driver just happened to be going in the same direction."

Vishal shook his head. "Buses are super slow and constantly stopping to pick people up. Nobody wants to be stuck behind one. They always change lanes and pass it. But the black car didn't." He tapped the car in the photo. "Do you really think someone with a car like this would be willing to spend miles sitting behind a bus?"

Zach looked at the sports car in the photo. "Yeah, I guess you're right. That's the kind of car movie jerks always drive."

Evie wrinkled her nose. "What do you mean?"

"Well, you know how a lot of times in movies there's kind of a jerky character? Like maybe a bully or a rude businessman or something? They always have cars like this."

Evie laughed. "I never thought about that, but you're totally right!"

A shadow fell over the table, and the three looked up to see Sophia standing in front of them, holding her lunch tray. Her face held an expression of cool indifference, but beneath it, Evie could see that she was nervous. "Would you guys mind if I sit with you?" she asked.

Zach immediately scooched over to make room. "Yeah, sure!" He smiled up at Sophia, but Sophia hesitated.

"Actually, I was wondering if, um, it's okay with you, Evie?" she asked shyly.

Evie's eyes widened. "Me?" She looked at the two

boys, who waited for her answer. "Oh. Wow. Uh, yeah, I guess so."

A relieved smile passed across Sophia's face, the first genuine smile Evie had ever seen from Sophia. "Cool. Thanks." Sophia picked up the paper napkin of her tray and unfolded it across her lap. "I mean, I don't have to sit here, obviously. I have tons of other friends I could sit with. Tons."

Evie held up her hand. "I get it, and I appreciate the effort. Don't turn around and ruin it, okay?"

Sophia smoothed her hair. "Right. Sorry." Everyone looked down at their lunches. Sophia nibbled on a carrot stick. "So, um, what were you guys talking about?"

Vishal exchanged looks with Evie and Zach. "Well, for one thing," he said slowly, "someone was following us yesterday."

"Someone followed us?" Sophia reached for the phone that Vishal slid across the table to her.

"Check it out." Zach pointed at the car in the two photos. Sophia bent down to look, and it was like an electric shock went through her.

"What is it?!" Evie asked.

Sophia bit her lip to try to hide the growing smirk that spread across her face. "You're not going to like this, Evie, but I'm pretty sure that car belongs to Evan Masterson."

***

After school that day, the four kids waited at the flag-pole for Sophia's driver to arrive. "Ugh, I can't believe it was Evan Masterson after all," Evie grumbled.

Sophia took a mock curtsy. "Told you!"

"Don't celebrate too soon," Zach said. "It's not one hundred percent certain it was Evan's car, and even if it was, we still don't know why he was following us."

"That's why we're heading over to my country club to check," Sophia answered.

"How do you know he'll be there?" Vishal asked.

"He teaches tennis there." Sophia made a face. "That's how he met my great-aunt." A black SUV with tinted rear windows pulled up, and she opened the back door. "Hi, Edgar," she said to someone inside. "I have three friends with me. Could you please take us to the country club?"

Zach nudged Evie with his elbow. *Friends*, he

mouthed silently. Evie rolled her eyes and gave her brother a good-natured shove. The kids climbed into the back and introduced themselves to Edgar, the driver. He wore a black suit with a crisp white shirt and narrow black tie.

Vishal grinned. "Oh, man, I've never been in a real chauffeured car before. I was kind of hoping you'd have one of those hats."

Edgar smiled back in the rearview mirror. "I keep one in the trunk for special occasions. Want me to put it on?"

Vishal laughed. "That's okay." The car drove along the tree-lined parkway, passing one old mansion after another, each with sweeping front lawns that looked out onto Lake of the Isles. It was a glorious fall day, and the clear blue sky and fluffy clouds were reflected perfectly in the still water. Joggers, dog walkers, and cyclists dotted the paved trails that circled the lake.

A short time later, the SUV turned onto a shaded side street and through a set of moss-covered stone gates. The road curved and led them to a circular drive in front of a sprawling white-pillared building.

Edgar pulled under the covered carport at the front entrance, and Sophia opened the door. "Thanks, Edgar. We should be ready in about an hour." The kids hopped out of the car.

"So does he, like, wait for you?" Vishal asked.

"Well, yeah," Sophia said. "He's my driver."

Vishal touched her arm. "Wait. You mean your *family's* driver, right? Not like your own personal chauffeur."

Sophia shrugged. "Why would my parents need a chauffeur? They already know how to drive."

"Yeah, no, obviously," Vishal said, shooting Evie a quizzical look behind Sophia's back. Vishal and the twins followed Sophia through the glass front doors and into the lobby.

"Where are we going?" Zach asked, looking around.

"To the back parking lot," Sophia answered. "It's right by the tennis courts." She led the others through a dining room and a wood-paneled bar area that was populated with gray-haired men and blond women in pastels, all talking about bogeys and pars.

"What the heck is a bogey?" Vishal whispered to Zach.

Sophia overheard him. "It's one stroke over par," she said with a sigh, as if it were the most obvious thing in the world.

"Yeah. That explanation? Not helping," Evie said.

Sophia sighed. "Whatever. It's a golf thing."

Vishal nodded. "Okay. Cool." The group continued through the back door and out into a parking lot. Several people in tennis clothes were walking out of the courts nearby, and Sophia dragged the others behind a hedge that lined the edge of the lot.

The group crouched down and peered through the leaves. The parking lot was full of cars, many of them luxury sedans and sporty roadsters. Vishal spied at least five black sports cars that looked similar to the one he had seen following them. "This is like finding a needle in a haystack," he whispered. "How are we going to know which one is Evan's?"

"That's easy," Sophia answered. She pointed to the lot. "Take another look."

CHAPTER
18

Sophia pumped her fist. "I knew it!" She turned to Evie. "I told you Evan was involved somehow! I mean, he had to be. The guy's a total dirtbag!"

Evie grimaced. "Okay, fine, you were right. Just out of curiosity, any idea how long you're planning to rub that in?"

"Mmm, pretty much forever," Sophia answered with a satisfied smile. Evie laughed.

"Where is Evan now?" Zach asked, looking around. Sophia led them closer to the tennis courts, staying low and ducking between cars. They peered between a gap in the fabric and saw a tanned man in tennis whites hitting balls to a blond woman in a pink tennis dress.

"Is that him?" Vishal asked.

Sophia made a disappointed sound. "No. He's probably in his office." She led them back into the elegant white building and through a door marked STAFF. The narrow hallway was lined with offices and framed old photos of people playing tennis and golf. Most of the office doors were open, and the kids could hear the clattering of computer keys coming from a few of them.

They stopped at a turn in the hallway and peeked around the corner. "That's his office," Sophia whispered, pointing to an office at the end of the hall. The door was closed, and there was a narrow line of light showing through the crack at the bottom of the door. The door was thin enough that they could just make out a man's voice talking on the phone. The kids pressed their backs against the wall and crept closer to hear better.

"I know you took it," the voice was saying. "I have proof. So either you pay me off or else!"

"That's Evan," Sophia whispered.

They could hear the tennis pro pacing the floor of his office. "Fine. I'll give you until tomorrow. If you don't get me the money by then, your face will be on the front page of every paper in the Twin Cities!"

The four teens silently exchanged confused looks. *What was Evan talking about?* Sophia crept closer, hoping to peer through a crack to see what Evan was up to. As she slid her back along the wall, she bumped against a portrait of a heavyset man in plaid pants. The picture slipped off its hook and crashed to the floor. The kids looked at it in horror.

Evan stopped pacing inside his office. "I have to go," he said abruptly. He hung up the phone, and the group saw the office doorknob begin to turn.

"In here!" Vishal pointed to a darkened office, and they ducked inside, pulling the door closed just enough to hide them from sight. Evan stormed into the hall, carrying a tennis racket. He paused beside the fallen picture, then walked a few steps down the hall toward their hiding place, his head bent forward like he was listening for something. The kids held their breaths, but Evan passed by the room and hurried off down the hall.

"He was accusing the other person on the phone of stealing something. Do you think he was talking about the North Star?" Evie asked.

"Only one way to find out," Vishal said. He ducked into the hallway, took a last glance to make sure they were alone, and pushed open the door to Evan's office.

The light was still on, revealing dingy cream walls and faded posters advertising tennis rackets from over a decade earlier. The scratched hardwood floor was covered with a cheap patterned throw rug that curled up at the corners. A build-it-yourself desk from a discount store was the newest item in the room, and the laminate was already peeling up from the top of it. A battered easy chair in the corner had an unzipped gym bag spilling over with tennis gear, and there was a half-empty bookshelf that appeared to function mostly as a dumping ground for useless junk. There were few files or papers of any kind, and no computer.

"Does he ever actually do any *office* work in this office?" Zach asked. "There's nothing here."

"I guess that means it'll be easy to search," Vishal said. He pulled out the drawers of the desk. "They're empty."

"Maybe there's something in his day planner," Evie suggested. She flipped through the black faux-leather datebook that she found on the desk. "The only thing in here is his tennis lessons, and he hardly seems to be teaching those at all. She held up the book to show the others. "Look. He only teaches five or six lessons a week. What does he do the rest of the time?"

"And more importantly, if he's not teaching, then how can he afford to drive this car?" Vishal asked, jingling Evan's keys.

"Good question," Zach said. "Keep looking."

Sophia dug through the cluttered bookshelf. She poked aside a pile of threadbare sweatbands and a dusty cassette recorder. "Seriously. Does this office have a single thing from this decade? Or even this century?" A stained golf ball rolled off the shelf and fell to the floor. She stooped to pick it up, and her eyes fell on something that froze her in her tracks. "You guys, we may not have found any evidence that Evan stole the North Star yet, but I can definitely prove he's a thief."

CHAPTER
19

Sophia pointed to an expensive gold wristwatch. "The inscription on the back says 'To Harold.'"

Zach looked thoughtful. "It definitely seems suspicious, but, I don't know. Maybe Harold was his grandfather or something."

Sophia's expression was triumphant. "I didn't read the rest of the inscription. 'To Harold, Happy Fiftieth. Love, Mar.' As in, my great-aunt Marguerite. Harold was her husband. He died about five years ago."

"Whoa!" Zach said. "That's weird. Any chance your great-aunt might have given it to him for some reason?"

"No way," Sophia said emphatically. "She adored my great-uncle; she still talks about him all the time. She would *never* give his watch away." Sophia used her phone to take a photo of the watch on the shelf before dropping both the phone and the watch in her purse.

"Sophia, what are you doing? You can't take that," Evie said. "It's stealing."

"He's the one who stole it from my family. How can it be stealing if I'm just taking it back?" Sophia asked. "Besides, it's evidence."

"Remember what happened the last time we brought evidence to the cops?" Evie asked. "It didn't go so well."

"It's not for the cops; it's for my great-aunt. When I show her this, she'll finally see Evan for who he really is: a gold-digging leech and a thief. I'm sure it's not the only thing he's stolen from her. And when she reports it to the cops, maybe they'll finally start investigating him for the North Star, too. I mean, he's got to be the thief for sure now. It all makes sense."

"I don't know," Zach said. "What about the phone call we overheard? It sounded like he was accusing someone *else* of stealing, didn't it?"

Sophia shrugged, unconcerned. "Maybe he was talking about something else. That conversation might not mean anything."

"Yeah, but if it *was* about the North Star, then it could mean everything," Zach said. "When my mom's working on a lead, she always says you can't just tell a story; you have to let the story tell you. Look at everything and see where it leads. If you pick only the evidence that fits your narrative, then you might miss the real story."

Sophia shook her head. "Well, my mom always says that if it looks like a duck and it quacks like a duck, then it's probably a duck. Evan's a proven thief, and he was at our house the night the necklace was stolen. It's not that hard to connect the dots."

"Let's see if we can find any more clues," Vishal suggested. "Maybe we can find some more stolen stuff, or figure out who he was talking to on the phone." He dropped to his knees and crawled beneath the desk, searching the underside. Evie felt along the bottom of the rug.

Just then, they heard footsteps approaching. "Someone's coming!" Zach whispered.

"What do we do?" Vishal asked. "There's no place to hide."

"Yes there is," Evie said, pointing. "Come on!"

CHAPTER
20

Evie grabbed the handle of the trapdoor under the rug and pulled it open. The kids scrambled down the ladder and closed the trapdoor, pulling the rug over the handle just in time. They crouched in the darkness, listening to the footsteps overhead. They heard the desk drawers opening and closing and someone rummaging through Evan's gym bag. A tennis ball bounced along the floor. Was someone else searching his office, too?

The sounds continued above for only another minute or two, and then the office door closed and the footsteps faded away. Whoever it was had been in a hurry. "Do you think it's safe to go back up?" Evie whispered.

"Let's wait another minute or two, just in case they

come back," Zach whispered back. The kids sat in anxious silence, waiting for any sound that would signal the searcher's return, but they heard nothing.

"Where are we, anyway?" Vishal asked quietly. "Is this some kind of storeroom?"

Zach waved his arm over his head. "Hold on. I think I felt something earlier." His hand found a string. He pulled it, and a bare bulb clicked on overhead. The kids blinked their eyes, adjusting to the sudden light.

When they got their bearings enough to see what was around them, Sophia's eyes sparkled. "Oh. Em. Gee. You guys, we found Evan's secret lair."

Vishal scoffed. "Settle down with the drama, James Bond. It's not a *secret lair*. It's just a . . ." He looked around more closely. "Oh, man. I think you're right. We are actually standing in a full-on secret lair right now." He prowled around the room, excited. "That is so awesome!"

The windowless storage room had been turned into Evan's second office, but this one was much more interesting than the one above. A long, expensive-looking metal dining table had been pushed against one wall and converted into a desk. A desktop computer with a huge silver monitor sat on one side next to a high-end printer and an open box of manila envelopes. A row of black-and-white composition notebooks were neatly organized between two crystal bookends at the other end of the desk. An array of expensive cameras and recording equipment sat on a shelf mounted to the wall. There were stacks of old issues of the local tabloid paper, the *Twin City Tattler*, piled on top of a row of fireproof filing cabinets on the other side of the room.

"What is all this stuff?" Evie asked. "Is Evan, like, a spy or something?"

"I don't know," Zach answered. He picked up one of the composition notebooks and leafed through it. "This has a bunch of initials and dates in it. It looks like most of them are from a few years ago. And then there's a column where he wrote 'paid' or 'won't pay' after each entry. See?" He held out the book to the others. The notebook was filled with neat rows of columns meticulously filled out in black ballpoint pen.

"The initials have got to stand for people," Vishal said. "Could these notebooks be for his tennis lessons?"

"I doubt he'd need a secret lair for his old tennis lesson calendars," Sophia said. "Besides, look how many people wouldn't pay. I mean, Evan's obviously a creep, but there's no way that many people would refuse to pay their tennis coach. Even a bad one. If his students hated him that much he'd be fired, for sure."

Evie ran her hand along on one of the filing cabinets. "Maybe these filing cabinets will tell us something." She pushed her thumb against the catch and pulled on the handle. The drawer slid open.

Sophia rolled her eyes. "Typical Evan. I mean, why put all this effort into building a secret lair if you don't even bother to lock your filing cabinets?"

"I guess he wasn't expecting anyone to find it," Zach said.

"And that's what makes him so second-rate," Sophia said. "He's too lazy to do anything right."

"Well, I'm just happy he is. Definitely makes it easier for us," Evie said. She thumbed through the files. "It looks like they're alphabetical. Hey, Zach, what's one of the sets of initials you found in that book?"

Zach looked down at the book. "Can you find a

GF in there?" He put the open notebook down on the table.

Evie pulled out a manila file with the initials *GF* on the tab. She opened it up and spread the contents across the table next to the notebook. Four heads bent over the contents.

"You guys, I think I know what Evan's game is," Vishal said.

CHAPTER 21

"Evan's been blackmailing people," Vishal said. He pointed to the file. "Look. GF is obviously Gwendolyn Fairbanks. He caught her lip-synching during one of her performances, and I think he tried to blackmail her. He held up the tabloid. "When she wouldn't pay, he sold the story to the *Tattler* a few weeks later."

"Gwendolyn lip-synched some of her performances? Wow! I guess that explains why she's retired," Evie said.

"And why she's always in such a bad mood," Sophia added. She picked up the other composition notebooks and quickly leafed through them.

"What are you looking for?" Zach asked.

"I want to see if my great-aunt's in here," Sophia said. "He must be blackmailing her about something.

Why else would she let him sponge off of her the way he does?" When she didn't find her aunt's initials, she tossed down the composition book in frustration and walked over to the filing cabinet. She opened the drawer marked *L* and pulled it open. "She's got to be in here!"

The others watched her with worried expressions. Sophia slammed the drawer shut and began opening random drawers, searching with a vengeance. "Where is it? Where's Marguerite's file?!"

Evie gently cleared her throat. "Sophia?" Sophia ignored her, and Evie spoke louder. "Sophia." Finally, Evie raised her voice. "Sophia, stop!" Sophia paused and turned to Evie, waiting. "Maybe your great-aunt isn't in here."

"What do you mean? She has to be!"

"Maybe your great-aunt just, you know, *likes* Evan."

Sophia scoffed. "Hardly! I mean, Marguerite's not stupid. The guy's a total loser! And now I finally know why she's wasting her time with him."

Vishal and the twins looked at one another help-lessly. Finally, Zach spoke. "Okay, fine. We'll help you look." The three searched through the drawers and notebooks, but there was no file for Marguerite LaFarge.

Evie bit her lip and looked at her brother. "What do we do?" she whispered.

Zach tapped Sophia gently on her shoulder. "You know what? I bet he took the file home with him. We should get out of here, though, before Evan gets back. We don't want to tip him off that we're onto him."

Sophia's eyes brightened. "Good point. We want to catch him red-handed. Evan Masterson: thief and blackmailer. He is gonna go *down*!"

Zach nodded. "The cops need to question him for sure. Because if he didn't steal the North Star, I bet he knows who did."

After Sophia took some photos for evidence, the four teens made their way through the trapdoor and snuck out of the office. Sophia led them out of the staff area and into a comfortable lounge with elegant sofas, floral-print easy chairs, and a crackling wood-burning fireplace. Evie pulled out her phone. "We should call Detective Bermudez," she said.

"In a minute," Sophia said. She walked over to a

carved wooden cubby near the front door where a uniformed receptionist sat behind a front desk. After a brief conversation, she returned to her friends. "My great-aunt's upstairs. Come on." She led them up a stair-case into a pink-and-green room with a wall of windows that overlooked the country club grounds and the lake beyond.

The room was full of old women sitting four to a table, intently focused on piles of white rectangular tiles clustered in the middle of each table. "What are they doing?" Evie whispered.

Sophia looked at Evie in disbelief. "Don't tell me you've never heard of mah-jongg," she said.

Evie was baffled. She looked at the two boys, both of whom looked like they had just walked onto a for-eign planet. "Have *you* ever heard of mah-jongg?" she whispered. The boys shook their heads.

Sophia sighed. "It's a game," she said with exagger-ated patience. "Sort of a combination of dominoes and gin rummy." When the others still looked confused, Sophia lost patience. "Why are you acting so weird? It's really fun!" She walked over to a white-haired lady in a pink sweater set. "Looking good, Elody. You think you're going to win?"

The old lady smiled at Sophia. "I'm going to take quarters from every one of these old hags!" The other women cackled.

"In your dreams!" one of her tablemates said.

"That's the spirit," Sophia said. "Have you seen Marguerite?"

Elody pointed to a table of three. "She must be in the bathroom."

Sophia nodded and patted the old woman's shoulder. "Thanks!"

Just then, Marguerite LaFarge appeared in the doorway of the Ladies' Card Room like a queen preparing to greet her subjects. Her helmet-like hair was dyed red, and her skin looked like marble. But in spite of her wrinkles and drawn-on eyebrows, it was clear she had once been a great beauty. She wore an expensive wool skirt and black silk blouse, and she was dripping with jewels.

"Sophia, my pet! What a lovely surprise!" The grande dame swept over to Sophia and embraced her, air-kissing her on both cheeks. "What brings you here?"

"I need to tell you something," Sophia said. "About Evan."

Marguerite sat down at her table and clucked her tongue. "Oh, that sweet rascal. What's he been up to now?" She plucked a tile from the middle of the table, looked at it, and traded it for a tile from the row in front of her.

Sophia knelt by her aunt's chair and pulled out her phone. "You need to stay away from him, Marguerite. He's bad news. I think he's blackmailing people!" She scrolled through the pictures she had taken of Evan's lair.

Marguerite waved her hand at her impatient grandniece. "Slow down, darling." She reached into her designer purse and pulled out a pair of gold-rimmed reading glasses. She turned to the other ladies at the table. "I'm sorry. You know young people and their phones!" The other ladies chuckled in understanding. "Everything's just so *important* to them these days!" She turned to Sophia. "Now what were you saying, dear?"

Sophia spoke louder. "Evan Masterson, Marguerite.

I think he's been blackmailing people." She reached into her pocket. "And he's a thief!" She put the wristwatch onto the table, facedown so that Marguerite could read the message on the back. "Look!"

Marguerite picked up the watch. "My Harold!" she cried. "Where did you get this?"

"From Evan's office. He obviously stole it from you, Marguerite! We need to tell the police!"

Marguerite reeled. "He stole my Harold's watch? Are you sure?"

Sophia nodded. "Yes, I'm sure. And it gets worse. We think he knows who stole the North Star!"

Marguerite stood up unsteadily. "Good heavens! If this is true, we must alert the authorities!" She gestured to a server carrying a tea tray. "Moira! Please escort me to the lounge so that I may telephone the police station." The server nodded and took Marguerite's arm. When she saw Sophia following behind her, Marguerite called over her shoulder. "Where is Evan now? We mustn't let him get away!"

"He headed out to teach a tennis lesson about half

an hour ago," Sophia said. "We'll see if he's still there!" She darted to the stairs, her friends following behind. They raced through the lobby and out the back door in the direction of the tennis courts.

When they arrived in the parking lot, the kids stopped in their tracks. "Oh no," Zach said. "We're too late." Evan's car zoomed onto the street, tires squealing. It cut in front of a minivan, causing the other driver to slam on her breaks and honk the horn. The black sports car peeled out and disappeared.

"Evan must have figured out we were onto him," Sophia said. "His car was moving pretty fast out of the parking lot." She threw up her hands in exasperation. "Shoot! How did he figure it out?"

"I bet it didn't have anything to do with you *taking his watch*," Evie said sarcastically.

"I told you; I wasn't taking it—I was returning it to Marguerite!"

"Yeah, I get it," Evie said. "But I'm pretty sure he would notice it was missing, don't you think?"

Sophia wilted. "I didn't consider that." She looked

helplessly around the parking lot. "What should we do now? Wait for the police?"

Vishal made a face. "Detective Bermudez was crystal clear he didn't want us investigating. If we stick around here we could get in trouble. Maybe we should, you know, lie low a little bit and see how things play out."

The others nodded in agreement. "Do you guys want to come over to my house?" Sophia asked. "That way if my great-aunt calls we'll be able to know what's going on."

"Great idea," Zach said.

Sophia called her driver, and the black SUV pulled into the parking lot a few moments later. Before they could climb in the back, Edgar hopped out of the driver's seat and hurried around the car, opening the back door with an exaggerated bow. He was wearing a black chauffeur's hat.

"Oh, hey, wow!" Vishal said. "Thanks!"

Edgar winked. "Didn't want you to miss out on the full experience." Vishal laughed and climbed in with the others.

It wasn't long before the black SUV arrived at the

ornate iron gates of the Boyds' estate. Edgar parked in the circular driveway, and the kids climbed out of the back. Vishal turned and waved before they went inside. "Thanks, Edgar!" Edgar grinned and gave him a quick salute.

Sophia led her friends to the kitchen at the back of the house. Late-afternoon sunlight streamed through the windows that looked out onto the pool and the grounds beyond. The white marble countertops and copper pots hanging from the ceiling gleamed. Sophia opened the refrigerator. "You guys want a snack?"

Zach looked at the others. "Sure," he said. "Can I help?"

Sophia shook her head. "I got it." She set a container of hummus and some cut-up vegetables on the counter and pulled out a big glass bottle of sparkling water. She handed the bottle to Zach and grabbed four glasses from one of the cabinets that lined the walls.

Evie looked out the back window, admiring the sparkling blue pool and expanse of lawn and gardens. "Your house is so pretty."

Sophia smiled. "Thanks!"

"What's it like?" Evie cleared her throat. "I mean, living in a fancy house and having servants and stuff?" She pointed out to the patio, where a worker in a baseball cap knelt at the edge of the pool, lifting the cover of the skimmer basket and reaching inside. Poles and assorted equipment leaned up against the wrought-iron fence that bordered the pool.

Sophia glanced out the window. "Weird."

"Yeah, it must be. Having so many rooms you could get lost, and having all these people around."

Sophia touched her arm. "No. Not that. It's just weird that we're having our pool cleaned today. Must be a scheduling mix-up. Our regular day is Thursday, but today's only Tuesday." She pulled out her phone. "Let me call Maurice and see what's up."

Vishal stopped her. "I don't think it's a mix-up. I think it's an imposter!"

175

CHAPTER
22

Vishal pointed out the window. "That uniform says A1 Pool Service, but you use Mermaid Pool Service. Unless Maurice switched companies, I don't think that's really a pool cleaner!"

The four teens ran outside, Sophia already dialing Maurice's number. They stopped a few yards from the imposter, approaching cautiously. He didn't seem to notice them. Instead, he was frantically pawing through the skimmer basket at the edge of the pool. "What's he doing?" Zach whispered.

"I don't know," Sophia whispered back. "Maurice says the cops are on their way." The teens crept closer. The imposter's shoulders were hunched and shaking.

Vishal narrowed his eyes, struggling to get a better

view. "Is the pool guy . . . crying?" Heedless of any danger, Vishal hurried across the patio.

"Vish, stop! What are you doing?" Evie hissed, grabbing his shoulder. He shrugged her off and strode forward until he was standing over the hunched figure.

The intruder looked up, and the teens gasped in shock to discover it wasn't a man at all. "OMG, it's Jasmine Jetani!" Evie cried. The YouTube star's baseball cap had fallen askew, and her long rainbow-colored hair tumbled out over her shoulders. Tears streaked her face, her heavy eye makeup melting down her cheeks.

"It's not here!" Jasmine wailed. She bent over the skimmer basket again, her hands scraping the edges of the basket. "It's not here!" She looked up pleadingly. "I swear I put it *right here*, and now it's gone!"

"What are you talking about?" Sophia asked.

"The North Star!" Jasmine cried. "I hid it here during the party, but now it's gone!"

Evie's jaw dropped. "*You* stole the North Star?" Her face clouded. "But you have tons of money! If you wanted it so bad, why didn't you just buy it?"

Evie's question seemed to snap Jasmine back into

herself. She swiped at the tears with the back of her hand and made a face when she saw the streaks of smeared makeup on her skin. "It wasn't about the necklace. If I wanted to dress like some wrinkled old has-been I could have bought that tacky thing a hundred times over. I did it for my followers!"

Zach stared at her. "Huh?"

Jasmine sighed impatiently and enunciated like she was speaking to a very small child. "My followers. Hello? Don't any of you subscribe to my channel?"

"I do," Evie chirped. "You're always doing the coolest internet pranks! Like last week when you did the furry flash mob that blocked off the freeway? Classic." Suddenly, her gaze sharpened. "Wait a minute. Are you saying you stole the North Star as a . . . prank?" Sophia looked stricken.

"I have the nineteenth-most-popular channel in the world. Do you know how hard it is to maintain that status? Hundreds of channels crop up every day, and each one has something newer and better. If I want any hope of getting into the top ten, I have to keep thinking of bigger and bigger stunts. What choice do

I have? So I came up with a stunt to steal the North Star. If I posted that video, do you have any idea how many views I would get?"

Sophia's face was livid with rage. "So you stole a priceless heirloom from my family, ruined our charity fund-raiser, and torpedoed the zoo's plans for a gibbon habitat just so you could get *more famous*?"

Jasmine blinked. "What's a gibbon?"

Sophia flew at her, hands curled into white-knuckled fists. Vishal and Zach grabbed her just in time. "Easy, easy," Zach said. "Let the cops handle it." He turned to Jasmine. "Where's the necklace now?"

Jasmine's shoulders sagged. "That's just it. I don't know! We had a perfect plan. I purposely spilled champagne on my dress, giving me an excuse to slip away from the party for a few minutes. Unlocking the safe with a magnet was a piece of cake. I dropped the necklace into my bag and climbed out the window onto the vase that D-Mack had put in place for me. I hid the necklace right here in the skimmer basket and slipped back into the party. I came to get it today, but now it's gone! I was going to return it, I swear!" Sirens wailed in the distance, growing louder as they approached the house.

"Liar!" Sophia shouted, struggling against Zach and Vishal. Black-and-white police cars pulled into the driveway, and uniformed officers streamed out of the cars. Maurice hurried from the door to greet them.

"I'm not lying!" Jasmine cried. "We had everything all good to go. The plan was to sneak the necklace back into the house, post the videos, and wait for the offers to start rolling in. D-Mack said there were a bunch of safe and security companies already lining up to sponsor my channel, maybe even get me my own reality show. He must have double-crossed me and taken the North Star for himself." Jasmine burst into tears again. "That loser! I should never have listened to him. I was set up!"

The police swarmed across the yard, closing in. "You're pathetic," Sophia spat. "Risking prison just to get more followers. You deserve everything you get." Officers surrounded Jasmine. Sophia turned her back in disgust.

As police started to drag Jasmine away, she brushed past Evie and grabbed her arm. She stared intently into

Evie's eyes. "987193. Find D-Mack," she said. "He's the key to everything."

The police yanked the YouTube star away from Evie and cuffed her hands behind her. As they ducked her head into the back of the police cruiser, she shouted over her shoulder, "Find D-Mack and you'll find the North Star!"

The police cruiser drove away, and the other officers loaded up their cars, several of them staying behind to talk to Maurice. Sophia bent over the skimmer, pulling out the basket and digging her arm deep into the hole. "There's definitely nothing here," she sighed.

"Well, it wouldn't be, not if D-Mack has it," Vishal said.

"If D-Mack even exists!" Sophia scoffed.

"He must exist," Zach said. "Who else would Evan have been blackmailing over the phone? It definitely wasn't Jasmine Jetani. She didn't want to keep the theft a secret, so why would he bother blackmailing her?"

"Good point," Vishal said. "Evan must have seen D-Mack take the necklace out of the pool skimmer when he was in the garden the night of the party."

"So everything just brings us back to Evan. Again."
Sophia threw up her hands. "And with Evan missing,
there goes our only clue."

Evie stared into the grass, eyes unfocused, her mind
turning over what Jasmine had said to her before the
cops took her away. Suddenly, her eyes sharpened as she
caught sight of something. "Not our only clue, guys. I
think Jasmine left us one of her own."

CHAPTER

23

Evie pointed to the selfie stick mixed in with the pile of pool equipment in the grass. "Look. It's Jasmine's cell phone. She left it attached to the selfie stick."

Sophia dove on it and pressed the home button before tossing it back down in the grass again. "Dead end. It's locked."

Evie picked it up. "When Jasmine was being taken away, she whispered a series of numbers to me. I think it might be the code to unlock her phone." Evie typed in the numbers: 9-8-7-1-9-3. The phone unlocked. "Bingo!" The others crowded around.

"Check her contacts," Zach suggested. Evie did a search, but there was no D-Mack listed.

"Maybe text messages?" Vishal said. He took the

phone from Evie and skimmed through her various texting apps. "Ugh. There are, like, at least a thousand open text threads here. It will take days to read them all."

"What about photos? Video? Maybe there's a clue there." Zach took the phone and scrolled through her photos. "Oh, wow. This is even worse. I've never seen so many photos and videos on one phone!" Image after image showed Jasmine posing by herself or with a constantly rotating series of other people. No one person appeared in more than a few pictures with her. "Some clue this is. Any one of these guys could be D-Mack. How are we supposed to figure it out?"

"There must be something somewhere," Evie said, taking the phone from Zach. "Otherwise, why would she bother leaving it behind for us?"

Sophia glanced over Evie's shoulder. "Maybe this is exactly why she left it behind. To keep us busy searching for this nonexistent mastermind, D-Mack, instead of helping the cops put her away and get the necklace back!"

"Oh, come on," Evie said. "Why would she make that up?"

Sophia rolled her eyes. "It's obvious. That way when the necklace went missing, she would have someone to blame. Think about it. If she did get caught, she could say she was planning to return the North Star but got double-crossed by her partner in crime, who took it for himself and conveniently disappeared. We go off searching for the mystery man, and she keeps the necklace for herself."

Evie shook her head. "No way. She was really freaking out. I mean, Jasmine may have a cool channel and all, but she's not exactly the world's greatest actress. I don't think she was faking that. D-Mack's got to be real."

"Well, there's only one other person we know who can prove that D-Mack exists, and that's Evan Masterson. But now he's taken off to parts unknown, too," Zach said.

Sophia's eyes widened. "Wait a minute. What if Evan *is* D-Mack?"

"Huh?" Evie asked. "How would that work? We heard Evan talking to someone else on the phone, remember? He said, 'I know you took it.'"

Sophia rubbed her hands together. "Yeah, but what

if there wasn't anyone else on the other end of the line? What if it was the whole conversation was just a performance?"

"Yeah, but for who?" Vishal asked. "There was nobody else in the room."

"For us," Sophia said with satisfaction. "Evan was following us, remember? He may have been spying on us in other ways, too, so he probably knew when we got to the country club. All he had to do was sit in his office, wait for us to show up in the hallway, and then stage a fake conversation for us to overhear."

Zach nodded his head slowly. "It does kind of make sense."

"I don't buy it," Evie said. "It seems like an awful lot of planning and effort just to trick a few kids. It's not like the cops are really listening to us or anything. Why would he bother?"

"The only way to know for sure is to find him," Vishal said. "And if anyone could guess where he went, I bet it's your great-aunt."

"Good idea," Sophia said. "The police have probably searched his condo by now, and I bet they'd tell her if they found anything interesting. Maybe they found a clue that shows where Evan went." She started walking around the side of the house toward the garage. "Come on. Let's see if Edgar can take us over to Marguerite's house." The others followed her, but when they reached the garage, the black SUV was gone. Sophia sighed in frustration. "Now what?"

Vishal and the twins looked at each other. "Uh, have you ever heard of the bus?" Vishal asked.

"The bus?" Sophia shuddered. "I don't think so."

"Oh, get over yourself, Sophia!" Vishal grinned and beckoned her down the driveway toward the street. "You'll be fine!"

**

A short time later, Vishal and the twins slouched in seats near the front of the bus, while Sophia stood next to them with perfect posture, holding the overhead bar and looking nervously around at the other passengers. Zach leaned over. "What are you doing?"

Sophia's eyes darted back and forth. "I'm looking for barfers."

Zach sat back. "What?"

Sophia explained. "Once when my mom was a kid, her nanny took her on a bus somewhere. The bus was crowded, but there was an empty seat. Since no one was sitting there, my mom took it. As soon as she sat down, someone told her that the seat was empty because the person it in before had barfed all over the place."

Zach gaped. "Your mom sat in barf without noticing?"

"Not exactly," Sophia answered. "Somebody had cleaned it up." She shivered. "But still . . . barf." She pointed to the empty seat. "Does that look barfy to you?"

Zach ran a critical eye over the seat. "I think you're probably safe," he said. Sophia reluctantly sat down.

Evie was leaning against the window, scrolling idly through Jasmine's phone. Suddenly, she sat up straight in her seat. "You guys. Check it."

The others crowded around. "What is it?" Vishal asked.

Evie held up a page of thumbnails on Jasmine's Instagram feed. "I think I just found D-Mack."

TheJasmineJetani
◉ Las Vegas, Nevada

392 likes

TheJasmineJetani
Thinking of getting my septum pierced
like my new BFF D-Mack!

Tammy_Wright
Go for it girlllll!!!!!!!!!!!

DanielBeastMode

CHAPTER
24

"Whoa!" Vishal pointed to one of the thumbnails. "She describes this bald dude as her 'new BFF, D-Mack.'" He tapped on the photo and expanded it, squinting to get a better look. "You can't see much, but he's got a goatee and some pretty intense eyebrows." He scanned the rest of the photo. "And a snake tattoo on his arm."

"Ugh!" Sophia rolled her eyes. "Seriously? A snake tattoo? That's so cliché."

"I don't care if it's cliché," Evie said. "We found him! That's awesome!"

"Well, we didn't exactly find him," Zach said. "I mean, we kind of know what he looks like now, but that still doesn't help us figure out where he is."

"Well, at least we know he's a real guy," Evie said. "Maybe we can send the photo to Detective Bermudez, and he can run it through a police database and see if they find a match."

"Can the cops really do that?" Vishal asked.

Evie shrugged. "They do it on TV."

Sophia looked out the bus window. "Oh, we're in Marguerite's neighborhood. She lives just down that street." Sophia pointed to a tree-lined lane with sprawling old houses set back from the sidewalk.

Zach stood up and pulled the bell string. "Let's get off here." The bus stopped, and the four friends stepped out into cool grays of the early evening light. The streetlights were just beginning to wink on.

"Do you want to call your great-aunt and let her know we're coming?" Zach asked.

Sophia waved her hand dismissively. "Nah. She's always happy to see me." After a few moments, Sophia led them up a steep driveway to a gray stone house with ivy growing on the walls. "Here we are." There was a long black luxury sedan parked under the old-fashioned carport, and a detached multi-car garage tucked in the back corner of the lot.

"That's a lot of cars for just one old lady," Vishal said.

"My great-uncle Harold was kind of a car guy," Sophia said. "He had this really cool old convertible MG that he used to take me out in on the weekends. It was so fun!" Sophia rang the bell, and the kids could hear the echo of melodic door chimes inside. After a moment, a petite young woman in a blue-and-white uniform walked down the front hall, patting her apron and smoothing her hair, which was pulled back in a tight ponytail. She looked through the window and smiled when she saw Sophia.

"Sophia, so nice to see you! Your great-aunt will be so pleased."

Sophia smiled. "It's nice to see you, too, Liana." She introduced her friends, and Liana led them down the hall to a sitting room with a dark-beamed ceiling and heavy, carved furniture. Every surface was covered with lace doilies and expensive-looking china vases. Gold-framed Impressionist paintings crowded the cream-colored walls. Although it was a warm day, the windows were shut tightly and the Batchelder-tile fireplace held a roaring wood fire. The air in the room felt close and cramped.

Vishal took two steps into the room, and his bulging camo-patterned backpack barely missed a crystal decanter. Evie grabbed his arm just in time, and she and the boys quickly removed their heavy backpacks and placed them carefully near the dark floral curtains that edged the tall windows on the far wall.

Marguerite LaFarge reclined on a brocade divan in the center of the room, an ivory afghan blanket tucked around her legs. She held a cool compress to her head, and a glass of brandy sat on the table next to her. When she saw Sophia, her mouth stretched into a thin smile. "Sophia, darling. How lovely of you to come and see me." She turned to the housekeeper. "Liana, we're almost out of brandy. Go fetch some from the market, will you? And buy some cake for the children."

Liana nodded and looked at the floor. "Yes, ma'am." She exited, closing the door softly behind her.

Marguerite turned back to her guests. "What a dreadful day it's been. I don't even know how I can face my mah-jongg club again."

Sophia perched on the edge of a wingback chair, and the others followed suit. "Don't worry about that, Marguerite. It's not your fault you were taken in by that creep."

"He really is the most awful rogue, isn't he? Stealing my Harold's watch like that! And blackmail, too? Why, I fell into a near swoon at the country club. They wanted to call the paramedics! Can you imagine the embarrassment? I refused, of course. Instead I called my manservant, Derek, and insisted that he take me straight home!"

Vishal leaned into Zach and made a face. *Manservant*, he mouthed. Zach bit his lip, trying not to smile.

"But you did talk to the police before you left, right?" Sophia asked.

Marguerite waved her hand dismissively. "That's all been taken care of."

Sophia leaned forward. "Have they searched his

condo yet? Have they found anything? What did they tell you?"

Marguerite grimaced like Sophia had done something distasteful. "Darling, you mustn't pepper one with so many questions. It's unbecoming of a lady. Hasn't your mother taught you that?"

Sophia's jaw clenched slightly. "My mother is a lawyer, Aunt Marguerite. Asking questions is kind of her job."

Marguerite let out a heavy sigh. "Well, I suppose not, then. Such a shame. I still remember the ball her parents gave when she was making her society debut." Marguerite shook her head. "She had such promise."

Vishal leaned over to Zach and whispered in his ear. "Did she just diss Sophia's mom? What's going on?"

"Don't look at me," Zach whispered back. "It's like they're speaking a whole other language."

Sophia's smile was brittle. "Last year, she was named one of the best trial lawyers in the Twin Cities. We're very proud of her."

Marguerite's smile was condescending. "Of course you are, dear. She is your mother, after all."

Evie broke in. "How awful this ordeal must be for you, Marguerite." Sophia looked at her gratefully. "I'm sure it will be such a relief for you when all of this is over."

Marguerite pressed her hand to her forehead once more. "To imagine that that cad Evan could take advantage of me like that, a poor defenseless woman! What kind of *monster* . . . ?" Her eyelids fluttered. "I shudder to think of how many other unfortunate victims he swindled."

There was a light knock on the door, and a muscular, clean-shaven man walked in carrying a lacquer tray. His hair was military-short, and he wore a black suit with a heavily starched shirt and a striped tie. He laid the tray on the coffee table. "Your tea, madam," he said. "Shall I pour?"

"That would be lovely, Derek," Marguerite said. "What would I do without you?"

Vishal stood up. "Excuse me, may I please use the restroom?"

Marguerite looked at him with disgust and waved her arm toward the door.

Derek picked up the steaming teapot and poured tea for Marguerite and her guests. Evie stared at his face, searching her memory. As he handed her a cup of tea, she smiled up at him. "You look familiar. Have you lived in Minneapolis long?"

Derek smiled politely and turned away from her. "I've only been here a few months. I just have one of those faces, I guess." He didn't look at Evie again and hurriedly poured the other cups. He stretched forward to pick up the tray and hastily left the room, closing the door behind him.

Once he left, Evie stood up. "Marguerite," she said softly, "I think you might be in terrible danger!"

CHAPTER
25

Marguerite put down her glass of brandy. "In danger? Whatever do you mean, child?"

Evie pointed to the sitting room door. "Your man-servant, Derek," she whispered urgently. "I think he stole the North Star!"

Marguerite's jaw dropped. "What on earth?!"

Evie showed the photo of Derek, and the group recounted Jasmine's story about the theft.

When Marguerite saw Jasmine's selfie with D-Mack, with his distinctive eyebrows and snake tattoo, she gasped. "Are you saying that my Derek is the same man as this D-Mack character? That he helped steal our precious family heirloom?"

Evie gave a solemn nod. Sophia gripped her

great-aunt's arm. "Not only that. We believe he might have masterminded the whole plot."

"Surely not Derek! You must be mistaken! He's been an exemplary employee since I hired him a few months ago."

"Did you find him, or did he find you?" Sophia asked. "It's possible he's been planning to target you next!"

Marguerite looked horrified. "Oh, good heavens! Have you told the police?"

Zach stood up and reached for the phone in his backpack. "Not yet," he said, "but we should call Detective Bermudez right away."

Marguerite stood up. "It's too late for that! Derek may already suspect something. We need to get out of this house and find help. He could be dangerous!" She tossed her blanket to the side and stood up, remarkably spry. "Follow me! But quietly, now. We don't want Derek to know what we've discovered." She picked up a set of keys from a bowl near the door and peeked down the hall. She turned back to the kids. "Now," she whispered.

In a panic, Sophia and the twins followed her without speaking, tiptoeing down the hall and out the back door, hoping they wouldn't be spotted. "Derek has the keys to the town car, but Harold's old MG is still in the garage," Marguerite whispered.

Sophia squeezed Evie's hand. "I knew she still had it," she whispered.

Marguerite led them across the dark driveway and unlocked a side door, flipping a light switch that illuminated a single bare bulb, which did little to dispel the shadows that clung to the clutter filling the garage. Two cars were covered with tarps, and piles of boxes, old gardening tools, and rusty paint cans filled the rest of the available space. Marguerite pointed to the dusty tarp on the far side of the garage. "Under there. I think I still know how to drive it. Quick! Go pull off the cover!"

The three kids ran over across the garage and tugged at the tarp covering the classic red convertible. A cloud of dust filled the air and fluttered down onto them. Zach sneezed. "Wow," Evie whispered. "I can't imagine a better getaway car." The little two-seater convertible was cherry red, with shiny chrome edging its elegant curves.

Zach grinned and elbowed his sister. "Not a bad way to save the day, huh? I hope we all can fit!"

Sophia grabbed his arm, and her voice dropped in horror. "Wait! We forgot Vishal!" Zach blanched.

That's when they heard the door lock behind them.

***

"Oh no!" Sophia cried. "Derek's locked us in! Quick, Marguerite—" Sophia turned to look for her great-aunt, but the old woman was nowhere to be seen. A look of fear passed over her face. "He must have grabbed her!" She ran to the door and pulled on the handle. "Don't you dare hurt Marguerite!" she shouted. "Do you hear me?" She banged on the solid wooden door. "Leave her alone! She's just a fragile old woman!"

Zach and Evie huddled together in the dim garage. Evie squeezed her brother's hand. Helping to find the necklace had felt like an exciting adventure at first. She had never imagined it would be dangerous, but now here they were. Held prisoner while their best friend was trapped in the house with a dangerous thief and a frightened old woman.

Sophia's eyes were wild. "Give me your cell phones. We have to call 911!"

Zach and Evie shook their heads helplessly. "We left them inside with our backpacks," Zach said, his voice weak.

Sophia slumped. "So did I."

Evie searched her mind for an idea. "What about Liana? She should be home from the market soon. Maybe she can call for help."

"Derek will be expecting her back, too," Sophia said. "Once she gets to the house, she'll be walking into a trap. We have to get out of here and find a way to warn her before she goes inside. It's our only chance of getting help here in time."

"Let's split up and search the garage," Zach said. "There's got to be something in here we can use to escape." The three spread out, rummaging through boxes, scouring shelves, and poking through piles of junk.

"Look for a spare set of car keys," Evie suggested.

"If we could start Harold's car, we could use it to ram through the garage door. That's what they always do in the movies."

"Evie, none of us can drive," Sophia said.

Evie shrugged. "We'd only be driving, like, a few feet. It can't be that hard."

"Sure, except for the part where we'd be *driving through a wall*." Sophia shook her head. "It's a terrible idea."

"Well, do you have a better one?" Evie shot back.

"I will," Sophia said, "if you just give me a few minutes to think of one."

"What about you, Zach?" Evie called across the garage. "Have you found a way out?"

"Not yet," Zach answered, "but I think I figured out where Evan Masterson went."

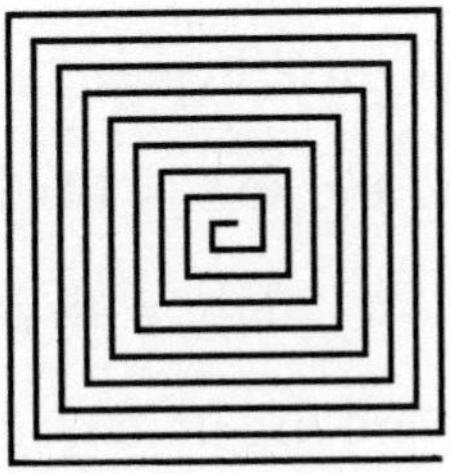

CHAPTER

26

"OMG, that's Evan's car!" Evie pulled the tarp off the second car, revealing the sporty black convertible they had seen at the country club, with its distinctive 10IS GOD vanity plate. "I don't understand. Is Evan hiding out at Marguerite's? There's no way she'd let him do that, would she?"

"Definitely not," Sophia said firmly. "She would never help anyone who stole from her. He must be working with Derek. Marguerite never drives anymore, so I bet Derek could easily sneak the car into the garage and hide it without her seeing."

"Yeah, but where's Evan now? I don't care how big your great-aunt's mansion is; she would definitely know if Derek were hiding someone inside her own house."

"Well, he must be nearby," Evie said. "Otherwise he'd take his car with him."

"We can worry about that later," Sophia said. "Marguerite's trapped inside with a criminal, and who knows what happened to Vishal? We need to find a way out of here and get help before it's too late." She pulled a stepladder out from behind a sawhorse. "Maybe we can use this somehow." She placed the stepladder against the garage door and climbed up, peering out the square glass window near the top.

"Is Liana back? Can you see her car?" Evie asked.

"It's pitch dark outside. I can't see anything."

"Let me see if I can find a flashlight," Evie said. "We can try to shine it outside." She squeezed under a workbench and pushed some boxes aside. Suddenly, she let out a sick-sounding yelp.

Zach ran over. "What is it?"

Evie backed up, her face pale. "Remember how we said that Evan must be nearby?" She gulped. "Well, I think I found him."

***

Sophia jumped off the stepladder and ran to join them. "Oh, my gosh, is he dead?"

"I don't know. Maybe?" Evie's voice was tiny. She held her stomach. "I feel like I'm gonna throw up." Zach put his arm around her.

"Let me see," Sophia said. She crawled under the workbench and pushed the boxes aside. Evan lay on the floor, his arms and legs tied up with ropes. His eyes were closed, and there was a flowered silk scarf tied around his mouth. "I doubt you'd bother to gag a dead person. At least I wouldn't," Sophia said. "It's not like they're going to scream or anything."

Evie gasped. "Sophia!"

"What?" Sophia looked at her. "It'd be a total waste of effort."

"That's not the point!" Evie said. "How can you talk about dead people like that? Especially in front of a . . . possible . . . dead person?"

Sophia untied the gag from Evan's mouth. "I need a mirror," she said, looking around. Zach jumped up and grabbed a crowbar. He pried the side mirror off of Evan's car and handed it to Sophia. "Nice one," she said, grinning at Zach. She held the mirror to Evan's mouth. It fogged up. "See? Not dead!" Her voice was triumphant. "The mirror fogs because he's still breathing." She felt around the back of his head. "He's got a lump on his head, but no blood. He must have been knocked unconscious."

Evie's face was incredulous. "How do you know all this stuff? You're like a murdery Girl Scout or something!"

Sophia looked smug. "I watch a lot of *Masterpiece Mystery!* with my parents."

Zach untied Evan's wrists and ankles and found some old coveralls to put under his head as a pillow. "So Evan wasn't hiding out here at all. He was kidnapped! I guess his blackmailing threats went too far, and Derek decided to make him disappear for a while until he had a chance to get away."

Evie bit her lip. "That proves that Derek's dangerous. He's already a thief, but now that we know he'll stoop to kidnapping, who knows what else he's capable of? We have to find a way to warn Liana so she can get help!"

The three stood up again. Sophia ran back to the garage door and peered out the window. She noticed the yellow squares of light shining lighting up the driveway just outside. She turned back to the garage and spotted something on the shelf. "You guys, I have an idea."

***

Meanwhile, Vishal sat hidden in the bushes in the front of the house, his cell phone in hand. After he had recognized D-Mack serving tea, he had excused himself and slipped outside to call Detective Bermudez. It had taken some convincing to get the detective to listen to him, and Vishal knew that a long lecture would be waiting for him and his friends when this was all over. At least he hoped so. He had no idea if his friends were still inside or if they had even realized that Derek was D-Mack yet. Vishal's stomach churned. Should he have stayed in the room and warned them? He hugged his knees, wondering when the police would arrive.

After what felt like hours, Vishal could hear the comforting sounds of sirens in the distance. They grew closer, and soon he could see the flashing blue and red lights as the cars pulled into the driveway and along the quiet lane in front of the house. Vishal was so relieved he wanted to run to them, but he stayed put.

Uniformed officers rushed past his hiding spot to the door and banged on it hard. When nobody answered, they broke the door down and rushed inside. Vishal picked up his cell phone and called Detective Bermudez. "I'm hiding near the front door in the bushes, and I'm scared to come out," he whispered. "I don't want the cops to shoot me by mistake. Will you come get me?"

"Where are you?" Detective Bermudez's voice was kind. Vishal told him where he was hidden, and heard the detective talking to other officers.

In a few moments, the detective's face appeared between the bushes, his face etched with concern. "You okay?"

"I will be once I know everyone else is safe," Vishal said, his voice shaky. "Are my friends still inside? Did you find Derek?"

The detective scratched the back of his neck. "Well, we're having a bit of a problem with that. I'm gonna need your help."

Inside the house, a cluster of uniformed officers crowded the entryway, talking in hushed tones and shifting from foot to foot. Over the creaking of their leather boots, Vishal could hear Marguerite's strident voice raised in irritation. He followed Detective Bermudez into the little sitting room, where they found Marguerite reclining again on her divan, wrapped in blankets and holding the back of her hand to her forehead like a heroine in a silent movie. His friends were nowhere to be seen.

A police sergeant sat beside her, notebook in hand, taking her statement. "As I was saying," Marguerite said, her voice heavy, "I've been through a terrible shock. I've just discovered that my dearest friend, Evan Masterson, was a thief and a swindler, and he's already absconded with some of my most prized possessions. I'm certain that he's behind the North Star theft as well. Why aren't you out finding him, instead of pestering me with useless questions?!"

The sergeant shifted in her seat, and when she spoke, her voice was patient. "I understand, ma'am, and we will find Mr. Masterson. But right now we're trying to track down one of your employees, a Mr. Derek Mackenzie, also known as D-Mack."

Marguerite waved away the question. "D-Mack? What a dreadful pseudonym! I would never have such a person in my employ. I have exceptionally high standards."

Detective Bermudez broke in. "We have witnesses who place Mr. Mackenzie in your home, Mrs. LaFarge. I understand you may be trying to protect what you consider a trusted employee, but it's very important that we find him."

Marguerite's voice sounded feeble, but her eyes were flinty. "I assure you, detective, if I knew of such a man, I would be happy to help you, but I have never employed anyone by the name of Derek."

Vishal was incredulous. "What are you talking about? Derek served us tea right here in this room less than an hour ago!"

For the first time, Marguerite noticed Vishal in the room. "Do the police make it a habit of bringing children along on their cases these days?" She gestured to the gathered police officers. "I assume this boy belongs to one of you."

Detective Bermudez's forehead wrinkled in confusion. "He claims he was here with his friends earlier this afternoon, and I found him outside in the front yard when we arrived. Are you saying you don't recognize him?"

"Certainly not," Marguerite huffed. "And he was skulking about in my front yard when you arrived, you say?" She narrowed her eyes. "That sounds like rather suspicious behavior to me."

The detective turned to Vishal. "Is there something you want to explain, Vishal?" He lowered his voice. "I know you and your friends are eager to find the necklace, but making up stories isn't going to help solve the case."

Vishal's eyes widened. "I'm not making anything up!" He cringed inwardly at how shrill his voice sounded, and forced himself to calm down. "I came here with Sophia, Evie, and Zach. Derek brought in the tea, and now he's missing and so are my friends."

He saw Marguerite shake her head in disbelief, and his voice rose again. "I'm telling the truth!"

Marguerite voice dripped with condescension. "Officers, there has obviously been some kind of misunderstanding. My darling grandniece did come to visit me earlier this afternoon, but I assure you she was quite alone. I had my maid, Liana, run her home about half an hour ago." She picked up the receiver of a landline telephone that sat on the table next to her. "Shall we telephone them to confirm?"

Detective Bermudez looked embarrassed. "I think it would be helpful, just to put everyone's mind at ease." He turned to the other police officers.

Marguerite's smile was pained. "But of course." She began to dial, very slowly.

The detective turned to the other police officers. "Looks like a false alarm, everybody. You can move out." The uniformed officers began gathering their things and trooping toward the front door.

"False alarm is a bit of an understatement, wouldn't you say, detective? Barging in on an old woman like this." Her hand fluttered at her heart. "We should all count our lucky stars I didn't expire from the shock!" She looked down at the phone. "Now, where was I? I'll have to start again, I suppose." She tapped the switch hook to disengage the line, and began dialing the number again, one button at a time, her eyes watching the police officers as they trickled out the door.

Vishal watched the exiting police with growing alarm. "Where are they going?" He tugged on Detective Bermudez's sleeve. "Search the house! You've got to find D-Mack and rescue my friends! He's going to get away!"

The detective held out his hands, palms up. "I can't search the house without probable cause, and there just isn't any evidence that Derek or your friends were ever here. Mrs. LaFarge says you were never inside the house."

"We *were* here!" Vishal insisted. His eyes searched the room until they landed on something familiar. He felt a surge of triumph. "And I can prove it!"

CHAPTER
27

Vishal ran over to the curtains and pulled them aside, revealing the kids' backpacks. "This one's mine," he said, holding up his camo-patterned pack. He unzipped the front pocket and pulled out his student ID. "See? That's me."

Detective Bermudez waved the officers back into the room. "Hold up, everybody." He stood over Marguerite. "Mrs. LaFarge, lying to the police is a very serious offense. It's clear this boy and his friends were at your house earlier this afternoon, and I'm certainly inclined to believe that Derek Mackenzie was here as well. I'm going to give you one chance to explain yourself, and if I'm not satisfied, you're going to find yourself in jail."

Marguerite pulled a lace-edged handkerchief out her sleeve and dabbed at her eyes, which were dry and clear. "I'm so sorry, detective, for telling a fib. This young man and his friends were here with my darling grandniece earlier today." She patted Vishal's arm. "I'm very sorry, dear, but you see, I just felt so badly for poor Derek. He's had a rough go of it, and I just hate the idea that he's been unfairly targeted simply because of his checkered past. He's an innocent man, and I wanted to give him a chance to escape and clear his name. I still can't believe he would truly do such a thing."

"I'm sorry to tell you this, Mrs. LaFarge, but Ms. Jetani's statement was supported by a multitude of evidence, including emails between her and Mr. Mackenzie. He was most certainly behind the North Star theft. Perhaps you've been a bit too trusting?"

Marguerite dabbed again at her dry eyes. "Oh, this is devastating news! I feel simply terrible for believing him. I gave him some money, and off he went. He could be anywhere by now!"

"Go track him down." Detective Bermudez nodded at two pairs of uniformed officers, who nodded back and hurried out the front door.

"What a foolish old woman I've been." Marguerite collapsed against the back of the sofa. "Thank goodness the other children went home earlier; I would be consumed with guilt if I had exposed them to any danger!"

"So the other children left," Detective Bermudez asked. Marguerite nodded.

"Without their backpacks?" Vishal asked, pointing at the floor.

Marguerite swallowed audibly. "Children are so forgetful, aren't they?"

Vishal's voice rose. "And without *me?*"

Marguerite stiffened. She closed her eyes for a moment. She opened her eyes for a moment and gave Vishal a kindly smile. "I'm sure it wasn't intentional, dear." She leaned closer to Detective Bermudez. "I don't think they care for him very much, poor thing," she said in a loud stage whisper. "You should have heard what they were saying about him when he left the room." She shook her head. "Children can be so cruel, can't they?"

"She's lying," Vishal said. "They're my best friends. They would never talk behind my back like that. They would never leave me behind."

"Wouldn't they?" Marguerite said, her voice sly.

"They must still be here, trapped somewhere," Vishal said, his voice firm. He stood up. "We have to search the property."

"Officers have already searched the house, Vishal. They didn't find anything," Detective Bermudez said.

"What about outside?" Vishal walked to the front door and turned back to the detective. "Will you help me look?"

Marguerite hurried behind him. "There's no need for that, young man. I assure you, they're all safe at home." Vishal ignored her and stepped out the door. She grabbed his arm to prevent him from walking down the steps.

Detective Bermudez hurried over. "I suggest you let go of him, Mrs. LaFarge." He nodded to the sergeant who had been interviewing Marguerite earlier. "Keep an eye on her," he said, pointing at the old woman.

Vishal and the detective walked outside. It was full dark, and most of the police had left. The remaining pair of cops outside were just closing the trunk of their patrol car and starting the engine. Bermudez tapped on the driver's window. "Hang on a sec; I just want to do a search of the grounds before you go." They hopped back out of the car. The group walked over to the side of the house and turned toward the back.

Vishal grabbed the detective's arm. "Look!"

CHAPTER
28

Bermudez and the officers ran over to the garage, where they had seen the message painted by Sophia and the twins. The detective banged on the door and rattled the handle. "Zach! Evie! Are you in there?"

They could hear Sophia's voice, muffled through the door. "Um, excuse me, but aren't you forgetting someone?"

Vishal's face broke out in a relieved grin. "Stand back, okay? We're gonna break down the door!" He took a few steps back and broke into a run toward the door.

Bermudez grabbed his shoulder before he could make contact. "Easy, tiger. Let's leave it to the professionals, okay?" He moved Vishal aside, and within moments, the other officers opened the door, and Vishal's friends came rushing out, all talking at once. "Whoa, whoa! One at a time!"

"Where's Derek?" Sophia demanded. "Did you catch him?"

"Not yet, but don't worry. We'll track him down. I have officers searching for him right now. The important thing is that you're all okay." The detective grinned with relief, but his smile disappeared abruptly when Evie grabbed his hand and pulled him over to where a weak and pale Evan Masterson lay on the garage floor, his eyes just beginning to flutter open.

Evie crouched down next to Evan and looked up at the detective. "When you do arrest Derek, make sure you add kidnapping to his list of crimes!"

"Where did he come from?" Bermudez asked, kneeling beside her. He put his fingers on Evan's wrist and checked his pulse. "Call an ambulance!" he shouted over his shoulder. One of the other cops grabbed her radio and hurried out of the garage.

"We found him in here," Zach explained. "We think he must have discovered that Derek was behind the

North Star theft and tried to blackmail him. Instead of paying up, Derek kidnapped him and hid him in the garage until he had time to make his getaway."

Evan's eyes blinked slowly open. He moaned and clutched his head. "But it wasn't Derek who stole the North Star; it was Marguerite!"

***

The group surrounding Evan froze in shocked disbelief. "Marguerite?" Sophia finally sputtered. "But that's . . . that's not possible. She would never do that! The North Star belonged to her sister. It's been in our family for five generations! There must be some mistake."

Evan's eyes closed for a moment. "It was no mistake. Two days ago, I was . . . well . . . I was looking through Marguerite's closet, and I found the North Star among her things. When I confronted her about it, she threatened me . . . told me to keep quiet or else. And when I asked for a little compensation for my silence, that's when Derek showed up." He rubbed at the angry red bump on his head.

"So it was Marguerite who locked us in the garage, and not Derek?" Sophia asked in a small voice.

"It looks like it," Zach answered.

Sophia swallowed thickly. "How could she do that?" Zach just shook his head.

Two EMTs arrived in the garage and put Evan on a stretcher. "We'll take the rest of your statement at the hospital," the detective told him. After Evan was taken away, Bermudez and the children walked slowly back to the house.

Marguerite had moved from the sitting room to the formal dining room. She sat regally at the head of the long mahogany table, just underneath a portrait of her late husband. When she saw the children, her expression grew defiant.

Sophia wiped at the tears that threatened to spill from her eyes. "So it was you all along? What about Derek?"

"Derek? That idiot couldn't plan his way out of a paper bag! He was merely a means to an end."

"But how did you trick Jasmine in the first place?" Evie asked.

"Oh, Jasmine, that utter fool! All it took was arranging for '*D-Mack*' to meet her at one of those ridiculous

YouTube conferences, and he had planted the idea in her head within weeks. She never suspected a thing. That empty-headed Barbie doll would do anything if it would make her famous!"

Sophia struggled to keep her voice from breaking. "But why, Marguerite? Why would you take the North Star in the first place?"

"Why indeed?!" Marguerite hissed. "It was galling enough when my mother left the North Star to my sister and not to me. I was the eldest; it should have been mine! And then when it was passed down to your mother, she didn't even have the courtesy to appreciate it. She was too busy going to *law school* and wasting time on *charities*. And then when your family decided to auction off our family history for a couple of filthy *monkeys*?! That was absolutely the end." She clutched at her throat. "Disgusting!"

Sophia's voice hardened. "Gibbons aren't monkeys; they're apes." She turned to Detective Bermudez. "Isn't this the part where you arrest her and drag her off to jail?"

The cops slapped cuffs on Marguerite's wrists and

marched her out the door. As she was leaving, she called over her shoulder. "The North Star has been in my family for generations, and you'll sell it over my dead body! I've hidden it in a place where you can never find it!" She let out a wild cackle. "Never! Do you hear me? *Never!*"

The kids followed the police out of the house and watched them put Marguerite in the back of a police car. "I'm not gonna lie," Vishal said. "It feels pretty good to see that. She is a nasty piece of work." He glanced over at Sophia. "Sorry," he said.

"No, you're right," Sophia said bleakly. She hugged herself. "I think 'nasty' is kind of an understatement." A black SUV pulled into the driveway, and Mareva and Dashiell Boyd jumped out, followed by Mrs. Mamuya and Vishal's parents. They ran to embrace their children.

"Thank goodness you're all right," Mrs. Mamuya cried. "We were worried sick!"

"I'm sorry, Mom," Zach said. "We were on a case, and it kind of got away from us."

"A case, huh?" Mrs. Mamuya mouth quirked into a half smile. "I didn't know I had a couple of detectives in the house. Maybe I should just call you the Gemini Detective Agency from now on, huh?"

Evie nodded. "That's actually not bad, Mom. I kind of like it." She nudged her brother. "What do you think?"

Zach grinned. "It's a pretty sweet name."

Mrs. Mamuya ran her hand over the top of Zach's head. "The next time you find yourself chasing down a lead, though, how about keeping me in the loop, okay?"

Evie hugged her mom tighter. "It's a deal."

***

A short time later, the police finished taking the kids' statements and walked them and their parents over to the car, where Edgar was patiently waiting, reading a novel. Mrs. Mamuya lagged behind with the officers, taking notes for the *Telegraph*. "My mom said the police found Derek at the Greyhound station, buying a ticket to Chicago," Zach said. "She heard it on her scanner app. They arrested him."

"Yes!" Vishal pumped his fist. "That's three down at least." He kicked a rock down the driveway. "But what's going to happen to Evan?"

"Once he's out of the hospital, he'll go straight to

jail, too," Zach said. "Blackmailing is a pretty serious crime."

"Good," Sophia said. "Although now that I know how awful Marguerite was, I'm kind of glad he was using her. They deserve each other." She sighed and looked at her feet. "I really wish we could get the North Star back, though. Marguerite said she hid it in a place we'd never guess. That could be anywhere."

"Man, that bites," Vishal said. "I mean, we kind of saved the day by catching the bad guys and stuff, but we didn't find the one thing we were looking for. *And* we still have to do homework."

Evie stopped in her tracks. "Homework? Oh, shoot! We left our backpacks inside!"

The four ran back to the house. A uniformed cop barred the door. "This is the scene of an active investigation," he said, barring the way. "I can't let you inside."

"But we left our backpacks in there," Evie said, "and we need them for school. Can we go get them?"

The cop sighed. "All right. Come on." The house was swarming with cops, who were checking under furniture, inside drawers, and even removing pictures from the walls in search of the North Star. Their faces were grim.

"I guess they haven't had much luck," Zach said, slinging his red backpack over one shoulder.

On the way out, Sophia noticed two officers searching the dining room. One was taking Harold's portrait off the wall. "Hang on a sec," Sophia said to her friends. She stepped into the dining room. "Could you guys please be careful with that? That's a portrait of my great-uncle."

"Don't worry, miss, I promise we'll be careful."

Sophia glanced around the dining room, drinking in its walnut-paneled walls, crystal chandelier, and Persian silk rug. "I always loved this room. When my great-uncle was alive, we used to dine here all the time. He always told the best jokes." She shook her head. "He would be so disappointed if he knew what Marguerite had done."

Evie's face broke into a grin. She reached out and squeezed Sophia's hand. "Don't worry. I think that pretty soon things will be looking up."

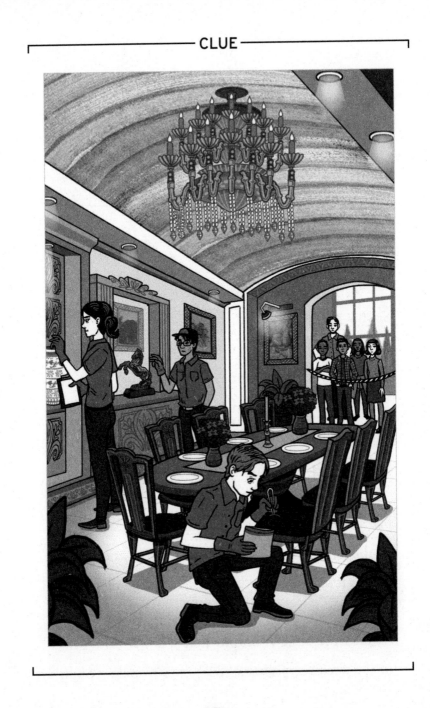

CHAPTER
29

Sophia looked in the mirror and tugged at the hem of her dress. She smoothed a stray lock of hair behind her ear and turned to her mom.

Mareva put her hands on her daughter's shoulders and bent down so they were almost nose to nose. "You ready?"

Sophia nodded. "I'm ready." Mareva handed her a black velvet box. Sophia popped it open and looked at the sparkling North Star nestled inside. If they hadn't found the necklace hidden in the chandelier, this day would never have come. Her fingertip gently stroked the large diamond that was the centerpiece of the necklace. "Thank you," she whispered. Sophia snapped the box shut and followed her mom through a set of double doors flanked by two guards.

"We're not taking any chances this time," Mareva said. The guards escorted them down a hallway and onto the ballroom stage of the St. Paul Hotel. The Gibbon Gala was packed with the Twin Cities' most prominent citizens, all dressed in elegant cocktail attire. An MC stood on stage dressed in a perfectly tailored tuxedo. On Sophia's cue, he picked up the microphone. "And now, the moment you've all been waiting for, the crown jewel of the Twin Cities and the highlight of our auction this evening, the incomparable North Star necklace."

A hush fell across the room as Sophia and her mother walked slowly to a pedestal at the center of the stage. Sophia opened the box, and the audience let out a collective gasp of appreciation. The diamonds sparkled under the stage lights. Sophia placed the box on the pedestal and stepped back.

"The bidding will commence at one million dollars. Shall we begin?"

***

Later that evening, Sophia found her friends standing near the buffet table. They were dressed in party clothes, and Evie's hair was freshly braided. "Wow, thank you so much for coming. You guys look fabulous!"

Evie hugged her. "Are you kidding? We wouldn't miss this for the world!"

"Besides, the food is amazing!" Vishal held up a plate piled high with food. "This is my third helping."

"Dude, I don't know if that's something to brag about," Zach said.

"What?" Vishal said. "I'm not ashamed." He pointed down to his too-short pants. "We bought these pants for all the bar mitzvah parties last year, and they're already too small. Clearly, I'm a growing boy who needs my fuel!" He took a huge bite of mashed potatoes.

"Where are your parents?" Sophia asked.

"My mom's over there." Zach pointed over to where Mrs. Mamuya stood talking with Detective Bermudez. "But don't worry, you can talk to her; she's not on duty tonight. She only reports on crime."

Sophia blushed. "Your mom's story on the North

Star was pretty awesome, actually. I think I'm starting to change my opinion on reporters."

***

A few months later, the families were all together again admiring the new exhibit at the Minneapolis Zoo. Gibbons swung happily through their new home, exploring every nook and cranny. A bronze plaque on the front read, *This exhibit made possible by the generous efforts of the Boyd family and their friends*. Sophia pointed at the plaque. "That means you!"

Vishal laughed. "As if! I think I only donated like ten dollars."

Sophia shook her head. "No way. Without you three, we would never have solved the crime and gotten the diamonds back. We could never have built this without you."

Evie put her arms around the other three. "We make a pretty good team the four of us, don't you think? With a little more practice, I bet we'd be unstoppable. I hereby declare that the Gemini Detective Agency is officially in business!" She let out a whoop, and the others joined her. Fascinated by the sound, the gibbons leaped to the front of their enclosure. One of the gibbons let out a cautious hoot, and soon its mate joined in. The song of the gibbons drifted out into the afternoon air, enchanting the crowd of visitors.

A tour guide stood in front of the exhibit. "Gibbons are known as 'the singing apes,' and now you can see why. With the help of zoos, conservation groups, and caring people like you, we will keep working to protect these animals and make sure their beautiful song will still be heard in the wild for generations to come." She pointed into the enclosure. "And as you can see, we're already off to a good start!"

ACKNOWLEDGMENTS

I wrote this book in the midst of moving to a completely new city and a house that had sat vacant for ten years before we bought it. I don't know what I was thinking, but I do know that I simply could not have pulled it off without the love and support of some truly extraordinary people. First and foremost, massive love to Kristin Hollander and Amanda Copeland, the truest, bluest friends a gal could ask for. Thank you for the big and the small and everything in between. I am also deeply indebted to the very kind and generous Dave Copeland and Jeff Hollander, who are almost as much fun as their wives. Heaps of gratitude to the gracious and welcoming Twin City kid-lit community, especially Heather Bouwman and Trisha Speed Shaskan. I love your books almost as much as I love the two of you. The writing scene here really is dreamy, and part of that is also due to wonderful places like the Loft and Red Balloon Bookshop. They do so much to celebrate writers, and I am deeply grateful for all of their support. To my locals, the Lowry and Liquor Lyle's, I don't think I could have finished this book without your quiet corners, free Wi-Fi, and BOGOs.

Much love to the Doran family for sharing your time and your country club with me. To the mahj crew, thank you for your spare change and for all the winds you keep giving me during the Charleston. This city has seriously been the loveliest, and I have felt absolutely embraced and welcomed by so many new friends and wonderful humans. Lucy Vilankulu invited me to every party, taught me to salsa dance, and introduced me to the divine Tami Lee. Ben and Lindsay Graves gathered me right into the fold and made sure I was part of the mix. Mary Grimstad-Ben Ari and Eylon Ben Ari always made my face light up. So psyched that our block has dear friends and neighbors like Katie Severt, Kim Cadieux, and Kevin Shannon. Sid Larson, Eric Van Oss, Matt Maland, Tony Dobek, Ji Cho, and Pam Liss have all been wonderful and gracious, and huge hugs to the embracing congregation of St. Paul's.

Many thanks to my former students and the other terrific people who inspired these characters, most notably Emmie, Lev, Matthew, Vishal, Tara, Brooke, Bella, Henry, Ana, Mareva, and Luz. I adore you all. And to all the teachers, librarians, parents, and caregivers who encourage, inspire, and support the children in your lives, you have my deepest admiration and gratitude. To my phenomenal editor, Sonali Fry, and the whole team at Yellow Jacket, thank you for believing in me and giving me the opportunity to write this mystery series. Working with you is a dream, and I have loved every minute of it. And Kevin Hong and Jomike Tejido, when I heard you would be illustrating this book, I felt like I'd died and gone to heaven. Your beautiful artwork is beyond anything I could have hoped for. To my wonderful agent, Erin Murphy, and my literary family at EMLA, I love and thank you one million percent. Enormous hugs to Elly Swartz, who continues to be the best of the best. To Mom and Dad, thanks for pretending not to notice all those times when I skipped swim team practice to read mystery books behind a tree. To the Fanueles, my deepest thanks and love for a friendship that has transcended even family. How lucky am I to hold you in my heart. And to Edward Gamarra, my dearest one, my gratitude for you knows no bounds. You are the compass that guides me home.